GONE

SHIRLEE McCOY

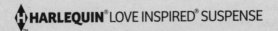
HARLEQUIN® LOVE INSPIRED® SUSPENSE

LOVE INSPIRED BOOKS

Recycling programs
for this product may
not exist in your area.

ISBN-13: 978-1-335-54386-8

Gone

Copyright © 2018 by Shirlee McCoy

This edition published by arrangement with Love Inspired Books.

® and TM are trademarks of Love Inspired Books, used under license.
Trademarks indicated with ® are registered in the United States Patent
and Trademark Office, the Canadian Intellectual Property Office and in
other countries.

www.Harlequin.com

Printed in U.S.A.

Sam glanced in the rearview mirror again and saw distant headlights. He accelerated, anxious to get off the two-lane road and onto the highway.

"What's wrong?" Ella asked, looking out the back window again. "Is that them?"

"Probably."

The distance between the two vehicles was closing. He floored the old Chevy, racing toward the entrance ramp to the state highway.

Headlights streamed into the Chevy, their pursuers edging closer. Someone leaned out the window and fired a shot. He felt the quick tug of a blown tire, fought to keep the truck under control as he flew onto the ramp.

A hundred yards ahead, an emergency turnaround split the wide median between the north and southbound lanes of the highway. He didn't brake, just spun onto the road, bounced across the median and sped in the opposite direction.

The other driver missed the turn, his brake lights flashing as he tried to stop. It would take a few minutes for him to recover and backtrack.

Sam had to find a safe place to pull off, and then he needed to make a call to his boss. She could put a team together and be in the area in a few hours.

All he had to do was make sure he and Ella survived until then.

Aside from her faith and her family, there's not much **Shirlee McCoy** enjoys more than a good book! When she's not teaching or chauffeuring her five kids, she can usually be found plotting her next Love Inspired Suspense story or wandering around the beautiful Inland Northwest in search of inspiration. Shirlee loves to hear from readers. If you have time, drop her a line at shirlee@shirleemccoy.com.

Visit the Author Profile page at Harlequin.com for more titles.

These things I have spoken unto you, that in me
ye might have peace. In the world ye shall have tribulation:
but be of good cheer; I have overcome the world.
–John 16:33

To Jude, Caleb, Seth, Emma and Qian.
You are my heart, and I am exceedingly proud
of the people you have become.

ONE

She woke to darkness so thick she thought she'd been buried alive. She shuddered, listening to the silence, trying to remember where she was, what had happened, *who* she was. Her mind was as dark as the place she lay.

She shifted, trying to ease a throbbing ache in her shoulders. Movement was difficult; her wrists were bound behind her back, her ankles bound, too. She should be terrified. She realized that, but all she felt was a strange numbness and the need to close her eyes and sink back into oblivion. Frigid air seeped through her clothes and settled deep into her bones, making her teeth chatter and her body shake. She'd freeze if she didn't move. Even that didn't scare her like it should.

If Ruby were here, she'd tell you to snap out of it.

The thought flitted through her head, and a million memories flooded in. The late-night phone call from the Damariscotta police telling her that Ruby had died. The frantic trip to Maine to identify her cousin's body. The hours spent praying desperately that the police were wrong. The realization that they weren't.

The grief that was still lodged beneath her sternum, throbbing in her heart.

She'd buried Ruby in North Carolina, and then she'd driven back to Newcastle to clean out Ruby's apartment. Two trips to Maine in two weeks, seeing the place her cousin had loved too late to share the experience with her.

It's inexpensive. Beautiful. Everything I've ever wanted. When are you coming to see it, Ella?

How many times had Ruby begged her to make the trip? Too many to count. Ella had always had an excuse. She'd always had a deadline to meet or research to do or some random obligation that kept her close to home.

Ruby, on the other hand, had never missed an opportunity to visit Ella. Christmas, birthdays, random trips just because.

She'd loved wholeheartedly and without reservation, and she'd never wanted Ella to feel alone. They'd been as close as sisters, the only living relative either had. Best friends, confidants and coconspirators in life.

And now Ruby was gone.

And Ella…

She was here. Wherever *here* was. Trussed up like a Thanksgiving turkey. Alone in a way she'd never been before. There'd be no one looking for her back at home. Her next article wasn't due for several weeks. Her neighbors barely knew her. Maybe, eventually, they'd notice her mailbox overflowing and contact the police for a well-check. If not, someone at church might wonder why she'd missed so many Sundays. By that time, Ella would be well and truly gone. A late-night docudrama—*The Disappearance of Ella McIntire*—watched by people all over the country.

She pushed the thought away, forcing herself to move. Her knuckles scrapped cold metal as she shifted to a sitting position. She trailed nearly numb fingers over the cold smooth floor. Not cement or carpet. Metal? Her brain was working sluggishly, but it was working again, her eyes adjusting to the darkness, taking in shadowy details of her prison. Silver-gray walls. No windows. No door. Just a dark alcove across from her that could have led to a hallway or an exit.

She needed to get up and get out, because someone had brought her here. Whoever it was could return. Probably would return. She'd been asking too many questions. She'd been talking to too many people. She'd been trying to find the truth, because she hadn't believed the coroner's report—that Ruby had died of an accidental drug overdose.

Ruby didn't take illegal drugs. She hated to take prescribed ones. She preferred holistic approaches to illness—meditation, healthy living, exercise. She rarely took an aspirin for pain and, as far as Ella knew, hadn't been sick with more than a cold in years. Her mother had died of a drug overdose when she was fourteen, and Ruby had vowed never to follow in her footsteps.

Ella had told the police that. She'd told the coroner that. They hadn't listened because Ruby had been found in her car, drug paraphernalia on her lap. Toxicology test had proven what had been obvious to the officers who'd found her— she'd died of an opioid overdose. That was a fact Ella didn't dispute. What she questioned, what she absolutely could not believe, was that Ruby had administered the drugs to herself.

So, while she'd worked on cleaning out Ruby's apartment, she'd talked to people who'd known her cousin. A social worker, hired by the county to work with recovering addicts, Ruby had met a lot of people. Ella had wanted to speak with all of them. In the few days she'd been in town, she'd done everything she could do achieve that goal. She'd talked to coworkers, to neighbors, to members of Ruby's church.

One of those people must not have liked the questions she was asking. Or, maybe, word had gotten out that she was making visits to the police, insisting that her cousin's death wasn't an accident. Newcastle was a small town. People knew each other. They talked.

Whatever the case, Ella had been at the medical clinic, waiting for a key to Ruby's office. She'd needed to remove her cousin's personal belongings, and she'd wanted to look for anything that might help her make sense of the tragedy. She'd heard footsteps behind her, turned and…

That was it. All she remembered. Her mind was blank. Just a black void that she was frantic to fill with knowledge, because she had no idea what had happened, how she had gotten here or who had brought her.

She only knew that she had to escape.

Something scuffled in the darkness. Fabric against metal or feet shuffling against the floor. She tensed, terror finally slipping through the numbness. Someone was there, she could feel the presence like an icy finger running up her spine. Whoever it was moved almost silently. Just those soft scuffling sounds mixing with the frantic pounding of her heart.

She managed to get to her feet, her ankles so tightly bound she could barely shuffle backward. Even if she could have run, there was nowhere to go. Just the dark alcove and the deeper, darker shadow moving through it. Her heart thumped painfully, her attention riveted to the person walking toward her. Tall. Broad. A man, she thought. But it was too dark to make out details of his face or features.

She yanked at her bonds, trying to shuffle farther away as if, somehow, she could disappear into the darkness.

"I'm not going to hurt you," the man said so suddenly, so unexpectedly, she jumped.

"Said every serial killer who ever tried to convince a victim she was going to be okay," she responded, her mouth cottony with fear.

"If I were a serial killer, I don't think I'd be worried about comforting you. Not when you're already bound and helpless."

"I'm not helpless." She glanced around, looking for a weapon, because she was helpless. Tied up. Alone. Probably far away from civilization.

"You are, but you don't have to worry. I'm not going to hurt you."

He was close now.

So close she could see his chiseled features—hard jaw, prominent cheekbones, light hair. Eyes that were looking straight into hers.

"What do you want?" she asked, still twisting her wrists, trying to loosen what felt like duct tape. If she could free her hands, she could fight. If she could fight, she had a chance of escaping.

"To get you out of here," he said.

"And take me where?" she asked. Not because she believed him. Because she needed to buy time. The tape was loosening, the edges cutting into her skin but slowly giving.

"Somewhere safe," he responded, grabbing her shoulder so quickly she didn't realize he was moving until he had her.

She yanked away, tumbling back and crashing into a wall.

"Calm down," he said, his voice low and soothing. As if that would make her more likely to cooperate. "I told you, I'm not going to hurt you."

"And I'm supposed to believe that because…?"

"Lady, if I wanted to harm you, it would already be done." He grabbed her shoulder again, and this time he held tight when she tried to pull away. "Turn around. I'll cut you free."

She didn't plan to cooperate, but he pulled something from his pocket. She heard a quiet click, saw a blade jump out and tensed.

"I'd rather not be stabbed in the back," she managed to say.

He sighed, swinging her around so effortlessly she barely had time to realize what he was doing before she was free. Her hands hung limp at her sides, pieces of tape still dangling from the skin, blood flowing back into her fingers.

He crouched, cut the tape at her ankles.

She tried to dart away, but her feet were numb, her movements clumsy. He snagged her hand and tugged her back. Not hard. Not with enough force to make her stumble. Just enough to pull her to a stop.

"Do you know where you are?" he asked.

"In a room with a guy I don't know who happens to have a knife. Let me go," she responded.

"You're twenty miles from town. In an old shipping container that someone converted to a building. It's sitting in a graveyard of other containers in the middle of a forest that would be very easy to get lost in."

"I'll take my chances. Let me go," she repeated.

"I have a vehicle. It's parked a couple of miles from here. We'll walk there, drive back to town and contact the authorities," he said as if she hadn't spoken.

"You either didn't hear me, or you misunderstood what I said. I'm willing to take my chances on going it alone." She tried to pull away, but he didn't release her.

"I think you're the one who misunderstood.

We're going together, because the men who brought you here aren't playing around. I'm not sure if they plan to kill you or sell you to the highest bidder, but I don't think either sounds like how you want to spend the rest of the night."

"Who are you?" she asked, running his words through her mind, trying to make sense of them. Kill or sell her? He was right. Neither of those things would be a good ending to her night.

"Special Agent Sam Sheridan," he replied. "I'm with the FBI."

"And you just happened to be hanging out in the middle of the woods right at the time when I needed help?"

"Not quite." He started walking, dragging her along beside him. She went mostly because she couldn't free herself from his grip. She still wasn't convinced his motives were altruistic, and she certainly didn't believe he was with the FBI.

"Then how about you explain how you got here at just the right time to help me? Because I'd really like to know."

"I'll explain. After we get out of here." He stepped into the alcove, pulling her with him.

It was darker there, but she could see a door on the far wall. Closed. He pulled it open. Cold air wafted in, and she could see moonlit trees and blue-black sky. Freedom. Just a few steps away.

She didn't give herself time to think. She shoved into him, using her weight to try to throw him off balance. He was a head taller and probably a hundred pounds heavier, and he barely moved. His grip on her hand loosened, though. Just enough for her to yank free. She bolted, rushing out the door, ignoring his shouted command to stop. One step into the cold evening, and then she was falling. Off a raised platform, tumbling toward the ground.

Sam snagged the back of the woman's flannel shirt, dragging her back onto the platform before she hit the ground. He didn't have time to be annoyed with himself for giving her an opportunity to escape. He certainly couldn't fault her for trying. In her shoes, he'd have done the same.

Only, he'd have probably succeeded.

She hadn't stood a chance.

Maybe five foot two if she stretched. A hundred pounds. Probably still trying to get feeling back in her hands and feet. She'd been bound tightly. Something he hadn't noticed when he'd seen her being wheeled off an elevator and into a parking garage at Damariscotta Medical Centre. What he'd noticed was her paleness, her closed eyes, how completely her body was covered by a blanket. He'd also recognized the man who was pushing the wheelchair. Mack Dawson was a low-level member of The Organization. Something Sam knew because he was a member, too. Deep undercover. Cut off from the FBI Special Crimes Unit he worked for, he'd spent the past month posing as tech expert willing to do just about anything for the right price.

He had a lot to lose if The Organization discovered him with the woman they'd kidnapped.

Namely, his life.

He was working alone. No well-trained team ready to back him up. The Organization, on the other hand, was multitiered and multi-membered with plenty of operatives living in and around Newcastle, Maine. Most of them were willing to commit murder if enough money was offered. He'd known that when he'd watched Mack shove the woman into the passenger seat of a small car. He'd known it when he'd made the decision to follow the car. Just to make sure the woman was okay.

He might be posing as one of the bad guys, but he couldn't shake the need to protect and serve. It had led him to work as a Houston undercover police officer and then to the FBI Special Crimes Unit. It had led him to Newcastle, Maine, and his assignment—finding proof that The Organization was kidnapping teenagers and shipping them to foreign locations where they were sold to the highest bidders.

Now, it had led him here.

To the middle of nowhere, trying to help a young woman who might be The Organization's next intended human trafficking victim.

Only, up close, with the moonlight falling on her face, she didn't look young or desperate enough. The Organization preyed on teenage foster kids. Troubled. Troublemakers. Family-less. The kind of young people who—when they went missing from their foster or group homes—were considered runaways. Currently, the total was fifteen kids in two years. All of them gone without a trace.

The woman he'd just freed from the shipping container didn't look like a kid. She looked to be in her mid-to late-twenties. Clean clothes. Professionally cut hair.

"What's your name?" he asked, and she frowned.

"Why do you want to know?" she replied, her voice thick and a little raspy.

"Because, I'd rather not spend the rest of the night calling you lady."

"Ella McIntire," she murmured, her gaze darting from him to the ground four feet below. "Thanks for not letting me fall on my face."

"Getting out of here would be a lot more dif-

ficult with you injured. Come on. The stairs are
over here." He turned to the left, walking down
five rickety steps and onto pebble-strewn dirt.
Several shipping containers stood in the weed-
choked clearing, their rusting carcasses blocking his view of the woods beyond. He didn't
like that. He wanted a clear visual of the surrounding area.

He also didn't like the fact that the shipping
container Ella had been left in had been set on
cinder blocks and fitted with a door that had
three locks and a dead bolt on the outside. He'd
picked the locks easily, and he'd slid the bolt
free, but he doubted someone inside could have
escaped. Not through the door, at least.

And that made him wonder if Ella was the
first person to be locked in.

Which made him think that she probably
wasn't.

And that made him want to call his supervisor, Wren Santino, and ask her to bring an
evidence team out. First, though, he had to get
out of the woods and back to a place with cell
phone reception.

He eyed Ella, wondering if she was capable
of walking to his vehicle. He'd parked a couple miles away, pulling his car off the road and
leaving it hidden behind thick foliage.

The distance itself probably wouldn't be a

problem, but they'd need to stay off the road, traveling through the trees parallel to it. That's what he'd done on the way in—pushing through thickets and crossing a small stream. Not an easy hike for a someone who already looked exhausted.

"I guess you have a plan for getting out of here. What is it?" she said quietly, eyeing the clearing. No expression on her face. No emotion in her eyes. Just pale skin and a few freckles, dark hair escaping a ponytail. Flannel shirt unbuttoned, a dark T-shirt beneath. Jeans. Boots. A splotch of what looked like blood on the side of her neck.

He frowned. "What happened to your neck?"

"I don't know." She touched her nape, and he took her hand, moving it so that her fingers were closer to the spot.

"There," he said. "It looks like blood."

"I still don't know." She shrugged as if it didn't matter. "You were going to tell me about your plan?"

"That's a quick switch."

"From?"

"You wanting to run away to you wanting to go along with my plan."

"I didn't say I was going along with it. I said I wanted to hear it. Because this place looks about as remote as anywhere could be." She turned a slow circle, probably taking note of the abandoned shipping crates, the weeds and trash littering the clearing, the thick forest that surrounded it. "And I'm not foolish enough to think I can find my way out alone."

"There's a driveway in," he said. "Just that way." He gestured to the western edge of the clearing. "But walking out to the main road on it isn't a good idea."

"You think the people who brought me here will return?"

"One person brought you here, and yes. I do think he's coming back. Probably with help."

"Help for what? Disposing of me?" She pulled her shirt tighter around her narrow frame, and he shrugged out of his jacket, dropping it around her shoulders.

"I don't know what they intend."

"You mentioned killing me or selling me off to the highest bidder. You must know something."

"I know neither of us wants to wait around to find out which option they choose. Come on. We need to get out of here."

"Do you have a phone? You could call the police. That would be a lot safer than trying to run," she said.

"There's no reception out here. We're too deep in the mountains. Put the jacket on. Let's go." He walked away, acting as if he expected her to follow.

To his relief, she did, hurrying after him. Taking two steps for every one of his. Dry grass crackling beneath their feet, cold wind rustling the leaves of nearby trees. It was early autumn, but it felt like early winter—a cold crispness to the air that reminded him of winter nights on his grandfather's ranch. Only back then, there'd been no villains lurking in the darkness. There'd been no hint of danger in the air. Those were the days when he'd been too young to understand how much evil the world contained, or how determined he'd one day be to protect people from it. They were also the days before his mother died and he was sent to live with his father. Forced to live with him. He'd have preferred to stay with his grandparents, but at nine years old, he'd had no say. The court had made the decision, and he'd had no choice but to abide by it.

The woods fell silent as he led Ella into the thick tree-line that bordered the driveway. He stayed far enough away to be hidden from any vehicles that might come along. Close enough that he didn't fear getting turned around or lost. The driveway was half a mile of gravel, deeply rutted from vehicles moving through. He'd taken a look after Mack drove away. Before he'd entered the shipping container and freed Ella.

He'd wanted to see if there was an easy way to block vehicular access to the clearing and slow the return of Mack and his Organization pals.

There hadn't been, and this was the best he could do—freeing Ella and fleeing with her, praying they could get to his vehicle before The Organization's henchmen returned. Low level thugs. Not the people Sam was after. He was after the top-tier members, the ones who called the shots and made the money. If he could bring them down, he could bring the entire Newcastle cell of the crime syndicate down with them. Blowing his cover wasn't going to help him do that.

He glanced at Ella. He'd give her credit, she was moving well, pushing through brambles and late-summer growth with grim determination. She'd done as he asked—putting on his jacket and zipping it to her chin. Her booted feet slogged through dead leaves and trampled dry branches. If she was tired or in pain, she didn't show it, and she didn't complain.

But, alone, he could have moved at double the speed.

His beat-up Chevy was well hidden. He wasn't worried about anyone from The Organization seeing it. Not until he pulled out from behind the undergrowth and onto the two-lane road that wound its way through a mountain pass and back to town. Once he was driving, his truck would be easily seen and recognized. The Organization kept track of its members. Where they lived. What they drove. Who they spent time with. He didn't want his truck seen anywhere near the location of their escaped captive. According to his paperwork, he was IT Specialist Sam Rogers, an old buddy of one of their low-level operatives, a guy who'd run drugs across the Mexican border during high school and college. Someone who might be willing to do anything for a price. He wanted to keep it that way.

But at the rate he and Ella were going, his cover would be blown before the sun rose.

"I'm slowing you down," Ella said as he held a thick pine bough and waited for her to duck under it. "Why don't you go on ahead? Once you get somewhere with cell reception, you can call the police to come for me."

"No."

"Why not? It's a sound plan, and makes a lot more sense than both of us getting caught."

"That's exactly why it's not a good plan. I'm not leaving you here to face The Organization's thugs alone."

"What organization?"

"The Organization is the name of a crime syndicate that has cell groups all over the country. Newcastle is one of its newest," he explained.

"What would a crime syndicate want with someone like me?" she asked, breathless, struggling to keep up.

"Funny, I was going to ask you the same question."

"I don't have an answer, Special Agent Sheridan."

"Sam. And most crime syndicates don't mess with people who aren't of benefit to the organization."

"Benefit? What does that mean?"

"Money. Favors—political or legal."

She snorted. "I'm a freelance journalist. I write human-interest stories for local newspapers and a few national publications. I also teach online writing classes for the community college during the fall and winter sessions."

"In Newcastle?"

She hesitated, maybe realizing she was giving away personal information and not sure she should be doing it.

"Not in Newcastle," he guessed. "You don't live in town?"

"No."

"Look, Ella. I'm sure you think you're helping yourself by keeping information from me, but I really do work for the FBI. I can find out anything I want to know pretty easily."

"I live outside Charlotte, North Carolina," she muttered, and he wasn't sure if it was the truth or a lie.

"And you're in Maine because?"

"My cousin passed away a couple of weeks ago. I came to clean out her apartment."

"I'm sorry for your loss," he said, offering a platitude that wouldn't do a thing to ease her sorrow. He knew that, but it was all he had. Unlike the other members of the Special Crimes Unit, Sam wasn't good or comfortable with the emotional aspects of the job. He'd been brought on board to work assignments like the one in Newcastle—undercover gigs that required someone who looked and acted the part the part of a criminal.

"Me, too," she responded. "But Ruby always said death was a beginning. Not an end."

"Ruby was your cousin?"

"Yes."

"It sounds like she had the right idea about things."

"She did." She fell silent. Not adding anything to that, her harsh breathing and stumbling steps reminding him that his pace was too fast for her. Too slow for him.

The soft rumble of an engine broke the silence, and she tripped. He snagged her arm, keeping her upright and pulling her deeper into the shadows.

"That's a car," she whispered, as if her voice might carry through the darkness and drift into the interior of the vehicle that was approaching.

Gravel crunched beneath tires, and lights illuminated the forest up ahead. Someone was coming down the driveway. High beams on.

He doubted the light would reach them, but he tugged Ella down anyway, crouching behind thick brush. She was inches away, her face a pale oval in the darkness, her eyes light-colored—blue or gray—and wide with alarm.

"What are we going to do?" she asked, looking straight at him.

"Wait until they pass."

"Once they do, they'll figure out I'm gone. Then they'll come looking," she replied, her voice tight.

"We're almost at the road," he assured her. "Far enough ahead that we should be able to make it to my truck without being seen."

"You would be able to if I weren't with you."

It was true, but separating wasn't an option, so he said nothing, just motioned for her to be still and silent as the lights drifted closer. They passed slowly, a few feet away, sliding across trees and bushes, and casting the world in yellow-tinged color. He could see Ella more clearly now, still just a few inches away, gaze focused toward the oncoming vehicle. Light brown hair threaded with red and gold. The splotch on her neck was dried blood over a purple bruise. A puncture wound of some sort?

The forest darkened incrementally. Gold to gray to nearly black, and he knew it was time to move again.

"Ready?" he whispered, but she was already up, sprinting ahead, pushing through foliage and disappearing into the forest. Heading away from the driveway, away from the road, deeper into forest that stretched for miles in every direction.

He followed, not caring about making too much noise or drawing attention to their escape. He had to catch her before she got lost in a wilderness that was just as dangerous and deadly as the men who were after her.

TWO

It was a mistake to keep running. Ella knew it. Just like she knew she shouldn't have panicked and taken off. Now she was committed to her escape—from the vehicle, the lights and Sam. The man who'd said he was an FBI agent. Who'd seemed to want to help her. Who'd probably be able to find his way out of the forest a lot more easily than she could.

She'd be lost soon, if she kept running.

Lost in acres of trees that blocked the moon and made her wonder which direction she was heading. Away from the driveway? Toward a road? Or deeper into the Maine wilderness.

There were bears here. Lynx. Moose. Animals that could maul, claw and trample a person. She'd researched the area before Ruby moved there. She'd been fascinated and worried by her cousin's decision to leave everything she knew to take a job in a state she'd never visited. Ruby had called it an adventure. Ella had never been adventurous. And she certainly had no experience in the Maine wilderness. If she got lost, she'd probably stay lost. But she kept running anyway, compelled by fear and panic and some instinct that told her being lost in the wilderness would be better than being found by whoever had kidnapped her.

"Stop!" Sam hissed, grabbing the back of the jacket he'd lent her and yanking her to a halt.

"And do what? Wait to be found?"

"Head for the road," he said, his voice so calm, she could almost believe that everything was going to be okay. "Right now, you're running away from it."

"And away from anyone who might be looking for me. That makes a lot more sense than running toward a place where I know there's danger." She whirled to face him, panicked, breathless, terrified. She hated that. She hated being vulnerable. She hated being afraid. She hated that she had no idea how to save herself from the situation she was in. She'd relied on someone else once. She'd trusted him. Jarrod had taught her everything she needed to know about how important it was never to repeat the mistake.

But right now, she wasn't sure she could go it alone. No matter how much she wanted to. She'd walked into something unexpected when she'd traveled to Newcastle. Or, maybe, it had been expected. She'd known—hadn't she?—that Ruby's death hadn't been an accident. She'd asked questions anyway. She'd pushed for answers because Ruby deserved to be remembered for the good she'd done, not for a drug addiction she hadn't had.

"We're staying off the road, remember? Just walking parallel to it. There's no danger in that. At least, no more than there is in running deep into a forest you're not familiar with." He had her arm and was tugging her back the way they'd come, his grip just firm enough to keep her moving in the direction he wanted to go.

"The lights of that car were too close," she said, her heart thumping wildly, her pulse racing.

"Not close enough for us to be seen."

"How do you know?" she responded as they neared the gravel driveway. She could see it through an opening in the trees—a few yards ahead, gray-white stones gleaming in the moonlight.

"We were behind enough brush to keep us hidden. Even if the light had been able to reach us," he responded.

"That doesn't make me feel better."

"Maybe this will," he said. "I don't take chances with people's lives, and I don't believe in unnecessary risk. If I didn't think this was the fastest and safest way to escape, I'd find another one."

She didn't respond, because there was nothing left to say.

She didn't take chances, either. She didn't believe in unnecessary risks. Not ever, but especially not since Jarrod. Somehow, she'd still traveled to Maine. She'd gone to the police with her concerns. She'd asked questions. She'd sought answers, and now, she was allowing herself to believe that a random stranger was trying to help her.

Please, God, don't let me be making a mistake, she prayed silently as Sam led her between towering oaks and narrow pine trees. They were moving more slowly now, taking a route with minimal undergrowth, their feet producing very little sound. Whatever the truth was about Sam—whether he was really with the FBI or not—she didn't think he wanted to get caught with her.

A car door slammed, and she winced, her blood running cold with fear. Soon, her kidnapper would discover that she was missing. Would he come looking for her? Or would he decide she wasn't worth the effort?

Another car door slammed, the sound so surprising she tripped and probably would have fallen if Sam hadn't been holding her arm.

"Careful," he whispered, his voice little more than warm breath against her ear. She had the strange urge to step closer, to hold on to his arm or his waist and make sure they weren't somehow separated. He might be a stranger, but he was there, and she really didn't want to be alone.

Voices drifted into the silence. Two men. Maybe more.

Please, don't let it be more.

Please, don't let them come looking for me.

Minutes passed as she and Sam picked their way through the woods, carefully, quietly.

"We know you're out here," a man called, his voice faint but clearly audible. "If you make us hunt you down, things are going to be harder for you than they need to be."

She might have frozen in terror if Sam hadn't still been holding her arm. His pace never changed, and he tugged her along with him. One step at a time, between trees, across a small stream.

"Ella McIntire," another man called, "you're going to die out there. Alone. Is that what you want? Come on back here. We'll help you get home."

"They know who I am," she whispered, the words slipping out before she could stop them.

"Shhhh," he cautioned.

Just that.

No words of comfort. No reassurance. But his steady pace was calming, his focus on what lay ahead instead of what was coming at them from behind reassuring.

Strange how much she wanted to believe he was one of the good guys and that he was leading her to safety. Maybe he was. Probably he was. Why else would he be helping her escape? What other possible motive could he have for freeing her?

Aside from Ruby, she hadn't trusted anyone in a very long time. Six years. She knew the exact day and hour she'd stopped trusting blindly. She knew the exact reason, too. Jarrod. Someone she'd loved without reservation. Someone she tried really hard not to think about anymore.

Something snapped in the woods behind them, and she jumped, glancing over her shoulder. Lights danced in the darkness, golden orbs sliding along the ground and bouncing off trees. One. Two.

Three.

She counted again. Just to be sure.

Three lights. Three people.

She tripped for the second time, her ankle twisting under her.

Sam pulled her against his side, whispering in her ear, "Careful. If you get hurt, I'll have to carry you out. That will slow us down."

She nodded and kept moving, ignoring the throbbing pain in her ankle and the hollow pulse of fear in her veins. She had to stay focused and play things smart.

The people behind them probably had weapons, and she didn't want to find out what they planned to do to her or to Sam. If what he'd said was true, he was an innocent bystander, an FBI agent who'd stepped in to help and who could lose his life because of it. Because of her. She didn't want that. She wanted both of them safe, but if only one of them survived, she'd rather it be him. She didn't want to live knowing that he'd died helping her.

She shuddered, wishing she could close her eyes, open them and find out the last couple of weeks had been a nightmare.

Actually, she'd be happy to learn that the past seven years had been a nightmare.

Voices carried through the darkness. Her pursuers weren't being subtle. They seemed to want her to know they were coming.

Maybe intimidation was the point.

Maybe they wanted to terrify her into surrendering or scare her into running deep into the wilderness. It would be easy to get lost there. Sam had been right about that. Just as he seemed to be right about staying silent and moving slowly. She didn't think their pursuers had any idea how close they were. Panicking and racing through the trees, breaking branches and making noise would have given away their location.

And it's exactly what she still wanted to do.

Run as fast as she could for as long as she could and pray they didn't catch her.

Sam pushed through thick undergrowth, pulling her up a ravine and out into a field of tall grass. A house had once stood in the center of it. She could see the crumbling foundation, an old fence and an outbuilding. She could also see the road—a gray slash in the lush landscape.

They stepped onto the cracked asphalt. She'd have preferred to return to the woods. At least there she felt hidden, protected by the thick tree canopy and dense foliage.

Sam didn't seem bothered by the lack of cover. He'd picked up his pace. First to a slow jog and then to a quicker run. He was moving fast, his longer legs eating up the ground at a speed Ella could barely match. Her lungs burned, her chest heaved, but she didn't dare ask him to slow down.

She felt the danger like she felt the cold air and the hard thump of her heart. It was there.

Right behind them. Every nightmare she'd ever had and all the ones she hadn't.

"This way," Sam said, yanking her toward the edge of the road.

She was certain she heard feet pounding on the pavement behind them. She didn't look. She was afraid of what she'd see.

A shot rang out, the sound reverberating through the stillness. A bullet slammed into a tree near her head, bits of bark flying into her face and hair.

She didn't have time to react. Sam dragged her into the foliage, pushing through brambles like they were air.

Another shot rang out, whizzing past somewhere to her left.

"Get down," Sam said, his voice clipped and hard as he swung around and pulled a gun from a belt holster. Smooth. Practiced. Effortless. As if he'd done it hundreds of times before.

She dropped to the ground as he fired three shots in rapid succession.

He dragged her up and into an all-out run before the sound faded away. He veered right, and she finally saw what they'd been running toward—an old Chevy truck tucked behind trees and bushes and hidden from the road.

"Let's go!" Sam opened the passenger door,

and she slid in, every nerve in her body alive
with fear and adrenaline.

Seconds later, Sam climbed behind the wheel
and turned on the engine, his gun hidden again.
He drove through undergrowth and sapling trees
and pulled onto the road. Three people were
standing in the center of the road. No flashlights. Just dark figures against the gray-blue
landscape.

"Get down!" Sam commanded as he forced
the truck into a one-eighty and accelerated. The
back window shattered, and she ducked, peb-
bles of glass falling onto the bench seat beside
her.

His truck had been seen. That meant his cover
had been blown. Sam wasn't going to regret it.
His priority was to help civilians—innocent
women, men and children who'd done nothing
to deserve the trouble they found themselves
in. Catching the people who preyed on them
was always secondary to ensuring their safety.

Of course, he was assuming that Ella was an
innocent civilian. He knew nothing about her
other than what she'd shared. For all he knew,
she was a member of The Organization and
had become a liability the higher-ups couldn't
afford to keep. Even if she was that, he'd have

helped her. No matter her story, he couldn't let her die.

Justice should only ever be served by the court system or by God. Individuals playing judge and jury were prone to quick and regrettable action. That had been drilled into Sam's head when he was a rookie cop in Houston. His partner and mentor, Mitch Daley, hadn't appreciated some of Sam's rougher edges. He'd helped smooth them out. Mitch was one of the good guys. Currently retired, he and his wife were spending their golden years cruising and camping and visiting their four kids and fifteen grandchildren.

"Are they gone?" Ella asked, lifting her head and glancing out the shattered back window.

"Yes." For now. Hopefully, for a while.

"That should probably make me feel better, but it doesn't." Bits of glass shimmered on her arm and shoulder, and he was glad she'd had his coat for extra protection. As it was, the bullets had come way too close to finding their mark. A second later arriving at the truck, a minute later escaping, and he and Ella might not have been so fortunate.

"The Organization isn't filled with people who want to make others feel better," he replied, accelerating around a curve in the road, putting more distance between them and the danger behind them.

"You keep mentioning The Organization. Why?"

"Because the man who transported you here was a member."

"I don't remember being transported, so I have no idea who he is."

"His name is Mack Dawson. He works as an orderly at the clinic—helping nurses, transporting patients from place to place."

"Okay."

"The name doesn't mean anything to you?"

"Nothing about anything you've said means anything to me. I'd never heard of The Organization until tonight. I don't remember meeting Mack Dawson."

"Do you remember why you were at the clinic?"

"I was planning to clean out my cousin's office. The door was locked, and I asked for a key. I was waiting for it. That's the last thing I remember."

"Your cousin worked at the clinic?" That seemed to be the center of syndicate activity. He knew of at least half a dozen people who worked for the clinic and The Organization.

"She had an office there. She was employed by the county."

"To do what?" he asked, pushing for more information despite her apparent reluctance to offer it.

He needed to know everything if he was going to help her.

"She was a social worker. She ran drug rehab groups and helped recovering addicts get back on their feet. She arranged haircuts and job interviews. She even drove people to appointments. Anything to get them away from their addictions."

"She sounds like a great lady." She probably had been, but that didn't mean she hadn't also been part of The Organization.

"She was," Ella responded softly, her words barely carrying over the whistle of wind through the shattered back window.

She was still looking in that direction, her left hand resting on glass that littered the bench seat. She had no visible tattoos. No rings. No jewelry of any kind. Not the normal Organization operative he'd met. He wasn't sure about the others. He assumed they were polished. Sophisticated. Well-educated. Well-dressed. Well-spoken. The kind of people who could easily convince others to do what they wanted. They had to be. They entered places like Newcastle and set up legitimate businesses that eventually served as covers for their illegal operations.

They hired people living on the fringe of society to do their dirty work, destroying families, homes, lives without a second thought. *They* were the people Sam wanted to bring in. Low-level thugs like the ones who'd kidnapped Ella didn't know enough about the inner workings of The Organization to help shut it down, but he'd be just as happy to toss them in jail, too. First, though, he needed to understand how Ella had gotten where she was—in the crosshairs of a crime syndicate that seemed to want her dead.

"Is it possible, Ruby was—"

"No," she cut him off.

"You didn't let me finish the question."

"You were going to ask if she could have been part of The Organization."

True. He had been. "Lots of good people get caught up in not-so-good things."

"Based on the fact that I was kidnapped, and we were both shot at, I'd say The Organization is a lot worse than not-so-good."

"What I'm trying to say—" Badly, apparently. Which was why he generally didn't conduct interviews with victims. It was why he preferred working undercover in very dangerous situations to interacting with people like Ella—people who'd been hurt, who were afraid, who needed sympathy and understanding. "Is that your cousin might have gotten involved in something that was much more dangerous—"

"And illegal and wrong than she thought? Not Ruby. She played by the book. Always."

"Okay." He'd broached the subject. Now, he'd let it drop.

"What does that mean?"

"It means okay. I'll take your word for it."

"Really?"

"I believe you believe what you're telling me. That being the case, there's no sense in discussing the subject."

"In other words, you think Ruby was part of a crime syndicate and that's why I was kidnapped?"

"In other words, I want the truth. Whatever it is, and whatever it means."

"There is no FBI field office is Newcastle, Sam. I don't think there's one in Maine," she said.

"There's not."

"I want the truth, too. Who are you really? Why are you here? How did you just happen to arrive on the scene in time to help me?"

"I didn't just happen to do anything. I was working undercover as an IT specialist hired to run the clinic's network system. I was leaving work for the day and saw you being wheeled into the parking garage. Something didn't seem right, so I followed the vehicle you were being transported in."

"You've left a lot out of that story," she said, finally shifting so that she was facing forward again.

"I gave you the truth. It's what you wanted."

"You said you're working undercover—"

"I was working as an IT specialist, taking payoffs from The Organization to manipulate certain computer systems at the clinic. The goal was to maintain my cover and gather evidence that would identify and lead to the arrest of top-tier operatives. Now, I'm working on keeping you safe."

"You don't have to keep me safe. You can drop me off at a police station and go back to what you were doing."

"No. I can't. First, because you're not going to be safe until you're far away from here. Second, because my cover was blown the moment this truck was seen."

"I'm sorry," she murmured.

"Don't be. My job requires that I protect and serve. I would have done this for anyone."

"I'm still sorry. What you were doing was important. Now, you can't do it anymore."

"We'll still bring The Organization down. We'll just have to go about it in a different way."

She nodded, her fingers tapping against the pieces of glass on the seat.

He lifted her hand, set it on her thigh. "I don't think you'll want to pick glass out of your fingers later."

"I don't want to be here, either. But, I am."

"Where would you rather be?"

"Home," she said, so simply and with so much longing he glanced at her way.

"That's in Charlotte, right?"

"Outside of it. Up until three years ago, Ruby and I lived a block away from each other."

"Is that when she moved here?"

"She got the job first. She'd been working as an addiction counselor at a Charlotte hospital, and she was ready for an adventure."

"You didn't want her to go?"

"I wanted her to be happy. Whatever that meant and wherever it led. Now, I wish I'd fought a little harder to get her to stay."

"You can't blame yourself for what happened to your cousin."

"Sure, I can."

"You shouldn't."

She laughed, the sound hollow and devoid of humor. "I'll keep that in mind."

"How was old was your cousin?"

"Thirty-two."

"So a few years older than you?"

"Yes."

"And perfectly capable of making her own decisions?"

She didn't respond.

"How did she die?" he continued, and she stiffened, her back going ramrod straight, her gaze jumping from the road ahead to him. He could feel the intensity of her stare, and he wondered what nerve he'd hit and why she'd reacted so strongly.

"A drug overdose," she finally responded tersely, and he thought she'd prefer the subject to be closed.

Too bad, because he planned to keep it open. Eventually. For right now, he'd let things lie.

He glanced in the rearview mirror and saw distant headlights. This was a mountain road that served a rural community. No one had been on it when he'd followed Ella's kidnappers in. He'd had to stay back and turn his headlights off to keep from being spotted. He found it difficult to believe that anyone other than the gunmen were traveling it now.

He accelerated, anxious to get off the two-lane road and onto the highway. It would be safer there. More traffic. More room to maneuver. More exits and entrances and ways to escape.

"What's wrong?" Ella asked, looking out the back window again. "Is that them?"

"Probably."

"They're catching up."

She was right. The distance between the two vehicles was narrowing. The old Chevy the FBI had assigned him for the undercover job wasn't fast. That hadn't mattered, until tonight.

He floored it anyway, racing toward the entrance ramp to the state highway.

The car was still gaining on them.

"Get down," he said, speeding around a curve, the exit ramp just ahead. Headlights streamed into the Chevy, their pursuers edging closer. He thought they might slam into the bumper, try to force him off the road. Instead, someone leaned out the window and fired a shot. He felt the quick tug of a blown tire, fought to keep the truck under control as he flew onto the ramp, rubber burning, the Chevy still shimmying.

He didn't ease up on the accelerator.

He couldn't risk having the other vehicle pull up beside him. A hundred yards ahead, an emergency turnaround split the wide median between the north and southbound lanes of the highway. He didn't brake, just spun onto the road, bounced across the median and sped in the opposite direction.

The other driver missed the turn, his brake lights flashing as he tried to stop. It would take a few minutes for him to recover and backtrack.

Unlike the rural route they'd been on, the state highway wasn't empty. Several big rigs zoomed past and a few RVs meandered along. The other driver wouldn't want to call attention to himself. By the time he found a place to turn without being noticed, Sam would be off the highway, the crippled Chevy hidden from view.

That was the plan.

Of course, he'd learned a long time ago that the best-laid plans didn't always work out. His relationship with Shelly was a prime example. He'd had it all figured out—how long they'd date, how long they'd be engaged, how big the wedding would be. She'd been in complete agreement. Until she'd met someone else and walked away.

He couldn't say he'd been devastated. Shelly had been smart and driven, energetic and funny. She was everything he'd thought he'd wanted in a life partner. She'd worked as an ER nurse at a hospital in Houston, and they'd met while he was having a knife wound stitched up. People had said they were the perfect couple, but she'd wanted a lot more than he ever had. More rooms in the house they'd buy one day. More expensive cars. More clothes, shoes and jewelry. After spending nine years in his father's home, all Sam had ever really wanted was peace.

The Chevy thumped along the highway, the

thudding flat making speed impossible. He needed to get off the road, and he needed to do it before the other vehicle caught up. He took the next exit ramp, thumping off the highway and onto a more rural road.

He had to find a safe place to pull off, and then he needed to make a call. Not to the local or state police. He had no idea if there were Organization operatives working for either. He'd call Wren. She could put a team together and be in the area in a few hours. That would push the odds of survival in his favor.

All he had to do was make sure he and Ella survived until then.

THREE

She didn't know where they were, but Ella didn't think it was far enough away from the people who were chasing them. A handful of ramshackle houses lined the narrow road they were traveling, lights shining from a few porches and seeping beneath several closed window shades. She assumed it had been a thriving community at one time. Now it looked old and tired.

"Do you know where we are?" she asked.

"About twenty-five miles from Newcastle. Maybe a little farther."

"And do you have any idea of how we're going to get back to town?" Because the idea of being stuck on the side of the road while three gunmen hunted them was terrifying.

"We're not. At least, not until my coworkers arrive to offer backup."

"I hope that's not going to take too long,

because I don't think we've got a lot of time to spare."

"It's going to be okay, Ella," he responded, turning onto a side road and turning off the headlights. No houses. No streetlights. Nothing but the grayish asphalt and moonlight. Even that seemed dimmed, the landscape dark and uninviting. The thumping sound of the blown tire and the whoosh of air through the back window filled the silence.

She had nothing to say. Because she wasn't sure it would be okay. She didn't know how they were going to escape this, and all she could do was pray silently as Sam maneuvered the dark country road.

"Do you think they saw us exit the highway?" she finally asked.

"I don't know. Let's assume the worst-case scenario. If we're wrong, no harm done."

"Assuming they saw us exit, what's the plan?"

"Stay a step ahead of them, and find a place to lay low until my backup arrives."

"Hopefully we manage that soon. The tire isn't going to keep rolling for long."

"It's not rolling. We're riding the rim."

"And?"

"We're not going to make it much longer, but we don't have to." He turned into a gas station, the once-brightly-lit sign dark, tall grass and weeds growing through cracks in the blacktop.

"I hope you're not thinking that we can get the tire fixed here," she said, scanning the lot and the darkened facade of what had probably once been a mini-mart. "The pumps are gone. This place has probably been closed for a decade."

"Exactly." He drove to the back of the building and parked so close to the brick wall that the bumper almost touched it. He flicked his wrist and the engine died; the truck suddenly plunged into silence.

She eyed him through the gloom, nervous and on edge, because she didn't trust him, shouldn't trust him, but she'd gotten into his car and allowed herself to be driven to a deserted location. Wasn't the number one rule for avoiding abduction not to allow yourself to be put in a vehicle?

She'd broken it.

She'd probably broken a dozen more safety rules, and now she was sitting in the darkness, looking at a stranger, wondering if he planned to take out his gun and shoot her. If she screamed, no one would hear. If she ran, she'd have to pray he couldn't catch her before she found a place to hide.

"Don't look so scared, Ella," he said, reaching into his back pocket.

She scrambled away, opening the door and trying to throw herself out of the vehicle. He yanked her back, his hand fisted in her jacket. She turned, ready to fight for her freedom, then saw the cell phone in his hand and froze.

"A cell phone," she said, and he glanced down at it.

"Yes. Did you think it was something else?"

"You're carrying a gun," she replied, and his lips quirked in what she thought might be a smile.

"Ella, if I'd wanted to shoot you, I could have done it while you were tied up and helpless. If I wanted to harm you, I've had a million opportunities to do so. I don't. So how about we agree that the safest thing for both of us is to stay in the truck, stay quiet and try to avoid attracting attention?" He reached across her lap, his forearm brushing her thighs as he closed the door.

He didn't seem to notice the contact.

She sure did.

It had been a long time since she'd been this close to a man. Three years since she'd allowed herself to be alone in a room with one. She'd been to a couple of therapists. She'd worked through the trauma, but she still had the fear. Way down deep, tucked away in the smallest room in her mind, she still had memories of the way fists sounded when they hit flesh. She still knew how much more painful a beating was when it came from someone who was supposed to love you.

She shuddered, and Sam frowned.

"Are you cold?"

"Yes." It was the truth. With the back window blown out, cold air was seeping into the vehicle.

He tightened his jacket around her shoulders without any fuss, muss or emotion.

"You must be freezing," she said, realizing she was still wearing his coat.

"I've got an extra jacket behind the seat. I'll grab it in a minute." He punched a number into the phone and lifted it to his ear.

She thought that she should tell him she didn't need the coat and return it to him, but she hadn't realized how cold she was until she was warmer. She burrowed deeper, inhaling the scent of pine needles, soap and something unmistakably masculine. There were no memories in that scent. Good or bad. Jarrod had always worn cologne, his hair groomed, his nails buffed. He'd been her financial advisor before they'd begun dating, helping her invest the inheritance her grandmother had left her. Rosemary McIntire had been frugal, and she'd known how to save. When she'd died, she'd had over a million dollars in stocks and bonds, another hundred thousand in bank accounts and two-hundred acres of prime real estate just outside Charlotte.

The land had been in the family for generations, and Rosemary had left it to Ruby and Ella. She'd split her money equally between them, and she'd left each a beautiful heartfelt letter.

The letter had meant more to Ella than the rest. She'd already had a job that paid the bills. She'd been living comfortably in a house she'd bought using her writing income. She'd never needed more than what she had, and she'd have rather had her grandmother for a few more years than a dime of the money she'd been left.

She'd told Jarrod that a couple months after they'd begun dating, and he'd told her that sentiment never made a person rich.

That should have been the red flag that sent her running, but she'd been smitten with his charm and charisma, excited by the passion he had for teaching classes at church, happy to have finally met someone who shared her faith and her life goals. She'd ignored that red flag and all the others that came after. When he'd proposed six months after their first date, she'd almost cried with happiness.

That had been the beginning of the end.

Jarrod didn't love, he owned. He didn't care, he controlled. All the little red flags became big ones as they'd planned their wedding. Eventually, it had all imploded. All the lies and the pretending and the gentlemanly facade had been swept away in a rage that forced her to see the truth. She'd broken up with Jarrod in person, because that had seemed like the right thing to do, and then she'd gone home.

Relieved instead of sad.

Celebrating rather than mourning.

She'd gone to bed feeling lighter than she had in weeks, and she'd woken to him yanking her from her bed, demanding that she tell him who the other man was.

Because, of course, there had to be one.

In Jarrod's mind, there was no way she'd have broken up with him otherwise.

She'd demanded he leave, and she'd called 911, but he'd been beyond reason, his rage and his fists leaving her beaten and bloody.

It had been terrifying. It had been horrible. She'd been hurt physically and emotionally. He'd gone to jail, stood before a judge, claimed that he'd lost his mind when she'd broken up with him, that he couldn't remember entering her house through an unlocked window or dragging her from bed.

She pushed aside the memories. Dwelling on them wouldn't change things. She'd made a mistake. She'd let her desires cloud her common sense. She wouldn't repeat the mistake. Ever.

Sam said something, his voice so soft she barely heard.

She glanced his way, realized he was talking on the phone. She heard bits and pieces of his side of the conversation. Something about the team and backup and trouble. An address. A question about arrival time.

So maybe he'd been telling her the truth.

Maybe he really was with the FBI, and he really had come to Newcastle to bring down an organized crime ring. Maybe he'd been in the right place at the right time and stepped in to help.

Maybe.

Probably?

She closed her eyes, trying to focus on his words, hear more of the conversation. The quiet cadence of his voice and the warmth of the jacket wrapped her in a false sense of security, and she could feel herself drifting away.

She wasn't safe.

Not with gunmen chasing after her.

But she couldn't make herself open her eyes.

She couldn't force away the lethargy that suddenly overwhelmed her. She'd been drugged by the men at the clinic. She knew that. She'd felt the sting of the needle, and then nothing.

Now that the adrenaline was gone, her heartbeat slowed to normal, she could feel the aftermath. Her thoughts were fuzzy, her muscles weak.

Fabric rustled as Sam moved, and even then, she couldn't open her eyes.

He tucked his jacket a little more tightly around her.

"I'm fine," she muttered, but she didn't push his hand away or give him back the jacket.

"I know," he replied. "Go ahead. Rest. I'll wake you if there's anything to worry about."

"If? I currently have more to worry about than I've had in all twenty-seven years of my life combined," she replied, her voice thick with fatigue.

She thought he chuckled, but she was already drifting on velvety waves of sleep, and the sound was as muffled and distant as her fear.

Sam glanced at his watch for the tenth time in as many minutes. It had been two hours since he'd spoken to Wren. Two hours since she'd assured him that she was sending backup.

Two hours with no sign of The Organization's men.

Two hours of waiting for something to happen.

He didn't like waiting any more than he liked sitting still.

He shifted in his seat, eyeing the empty lot.

He wanted to think he'd lost the men who'd been following them, but The Organization was currently the largest crime syndicate in the US, its tentacles stretching as far south as Florida and as far west as Ohio. It may have expanded farther than that, but the FBI had no current information on West Coast operations.

What they had were dozens of small cells that had been busted by hardworking agents. As fast as they shut one down, another one formed.

Up until five months ago, Sam had known nothing about The Organization. Sure, he'd heard rumors. He knew it existed and that other federal agents were working to shut it down, but he'd only been vaguely aware of how it functioned. And then he'd heard about a similar case in Boston.

There, a social worker had contacted the FBI asking for help in locating several missing teenagers. They were kids the police said were runaways. She believed they'd been harmed. Seventeen foster children between the ages of thirteen and eighteen. Mistreated. Abused. Neglected. Removed from bad situations and, often, placed in worse ones. The social worker had known most of them for years, and she didn't think any of them would want to disappear so thoroughly. No contact with friends. No sign of them for weeks and then months. All of them just…gone.

She'd approached the Boston police and her concerns had been brushed off, so she'd brought the files to the FBI. One year. Seventeen supposed runaways who'd disappeared without a trace.

The agent she'd met with had agreed it didn't add up, and he'd passed the case on to the Special Crimes Unit.

That had been the beginning.

Then a guy named Bo Williams contacted the FBI to report a human trafficking ring. At first, the accusations were ignored. Bo was a small-time criminal with a history of drug dealing and weapons violations. His testimony was suspect, but he'd insisted he had proof. When he'd mentioned foster kids being preyed on, it raised an alarm that rang clear and loud right to the Special Crimes Unit.

Wren had invited him to visit the Boston field office. Her meeting with him had been informative. She'd gathered enough information to know he'd been on The Organization's payroll for a couple of years. He'd laundered money for them through a pawnshop he had in Newcastle, Maine. The pay was good, but his contacts in the crime ring were pushing him to get involved in something darker. They wanted him to offer jobs to certain teenage runaways. They had lists of names that he thought had come from a medical clinic in the area, and when three of those kids showed up looking for work, he'd hired them.

Four months.

Three kids.

They'd all been hard workers who'd been happy for employment, and every one of them had walked away from the job before their first paycheck was issued.

In Bo's mind, there could be no other explanation—The Organization was trafficking humans. If his suspicions were correct, someone at the clinic compiled the names of potential victims—young people who were drifters and runaways, who had no family looking out for them, no network of support that would be concerned if they suddenly disappeared. They were using private medical information to prey on unsuspecting kids. Bo hadn't been willing to be part of that.

He also hadn't been willing to die.

Which is what would have happened if he'd defected from The Organization. Leaving, running, trying to hide could only end one way. His death. The Organization didn't let members quit. Ever. He knew that, and so he'd approached the FBI, determined to stop whoever was calling the shots in Newcastle.

Wren had agreed to help him do that. She'd met with the team, gone over the information and outlined a plan that would help them obtain everything they needed to shut down the Newcastle Organization cell.

Sam had been that plan. Bo had offered his name to a few contacts in The Organization. Within a month, Sam had been offered a job as an IT specialist at the medical clinic. Sam wasn't the computer expert on the team, Honor Remington was, but he had a Southern accent that matched Bo's. That would make the story Bo told easier to believe—they'd grown up next door to each other in a small town on the Mexican border. They'd been drug-running buddies while they were in high school, and they'd broken the law together more times than they'd kept it.

Honor had coached him in the weeks prior to his move to Newcastle, giving him a crash course in computer networking. Her main job, though, was to trace the origin of the emails Sam had been receiving. The unsolicited job offer. The communication back and forth from that. None of those had come from the medical clinic, but a week after communication had begun, the HR person had called and asked him to report for work the following Monday. Once he'd agreed and moved to Newcastle, there'd been other emails. One of them had been a request to install specialized software into the clinic's mainframe. Someone had sent those things. Once they knew who, they might be able to find out why. If Bo was right, they'd take the perpetrators down.

Like Sam, Honor was in town, but she wasn't trying to infiltrate The Organization. She was teaching tech classes at a local community college, keeping it low-key and using software she'd developed to try to go in through the back door of the computer that had sent the emails to Sam.

Thus far, she hadn't been successful.

Whoever the person was had his computer and accounts well guarded. Honor wasn't letting that stop her. She'd been a hacker when she was a teen, busting down firewalls and infiltrating school and government systems. Not to cause trouble. To see if she could. Every system had weaknesses, and now she got paid to exploit them.

Sam knew she loved what she did.

He also knew that she'd eventually find a way into the anonymous emailer's computer.

He wasn't sure how close she was. They were no-contact in an effort to keep The Organization from making connections between them. Any information Sam had about the work Honor was doing, he'd gotten secondhand from Wren during their weekly check-ins.

Now, with his cover blown and The Organization's thugs coming after him, no-contact was out the window. Wren had called Honor and asked her to make the drive from town to Sam's location.

She should have arrived over an hour ago.

He glanced at his watch again and frowned, pulling out his phone and dialing Honor's number.

She answered almost immediately.

"I was wondering if you'd call," she said. "I would have contacted you, but I didn't want to buzz your phone. Distracting you in the middle of an epic gun battle wouldn't have been a good thing."

"How often do we have epic gun battles, Honor?" he asked, amused by her the way he always was. She was the youngest member of the unit—recruited just after she'd completed a PhD program at MIT. She had no background in law enforcement, but what she lacked in experience she made up for in eagerness to learn.

"I can't remember there being one since I joined the unit, but that doesn't mean they don't happen. Statistically—"

"Statistically, you should have been here an hour and a half ago," he cut in, knowing she'd give him every statistic about gunfights and law enforcement that she'd ever read. Knowing her, that would be a lot. She had a photographic memory and a serious yen for trivia.

"Statistics mean nothing when an agent is faced with a police blockade. I've spent the past ninety minutes sitting on the state highway in a line of traffic two-point-three miles away from the exit I'm supposed to take."

"There's a police blockade?"

"I'm pretty sure that's what I said, Sam. I can't see it from my position, but a trucker in a semi next to me walked to the front of the traffic line and checked things out."

"Did he speak with the police?"

"Yes. They told him a Damariscotta bank was robbed at gunpoint. They have reason to believe the perpetrator is from Newcastle and is heading back home. They're sorry for the inconvenience, but they have to protect their citizens."

"That's noble of them."

"Yeah. Interesting side note—the perp they described looked a lot like you. Tall. Muscular. Blond."

"Yeah. Interesting," he replied. "What else did the trucker find out?"

"The guy might be traveling with a woman,

and if anyone sees them, they're armed and dangerous, so the local authorities should be called and no contact should be made."

"So I've got an entire town looking for me."

"Doubtful. I've been in Newcastle for a few weeks, and the nightlife there is dead. The people sitting on this road tonight are truckers or travelers. Most of them are anyway. I'm sure there are outliers. If there are three dozen cars, maybe one or two will be from Newcastle. Tops that's a few townspeople."

"Plus the police officers who are conducting the search, and they're the only ones we need to worry about," he pointed out. "I'm glad I went with my gut and called Wren for backup rather than the local PD. Maybe you can get badge numbers and names when you reach the blockade."

"If I ever do. At the rate traffic is moving, my next birthday could come and go before I reach the front of the line."

"Your birthday isn't until March," he said.

"My point exactly."

"I'd rather have you here well before then, but at least the blockade clarifies some things."

"Like the fact that I don't like sitting in traffic?" she grumbled.

"Like the fact that the local police have a couple of officers who are working for The Organization."

"Or The Organization has a couple of operatives who are really good at pretending to be cops. That happens, Sam. I've read dozens of stories about ordinary citizens being duped by wolves in cops' clothing."

"I'm not sure which scenario I think is more likely."

"Don't use your brainpower trying to figure it out. Wren is already on it. I called her an hour ago. She's been trying to reach local authorities to ask about the blockade. The dispatcher assured her that the sheriff would contact her shortly, but she hasn't heard from him. I think she's decided to try the state police. They might be able to verify or refute the armed robber story."

"It's going to be interesting to see what the sheriff says about this. If he's avoiding Wren's call, he's going to have to explain why. If the dispatcher didn't pass along the message, that's an entirely different situation."

"Either way, I think it's safe to assume someone at the police department is working for The Organization. The way I see it… Hold on." She paused. "Looks like there's a state police cruiser coming up at the rear of the line. Lights flashing, but no siren. He's riding the left shoulder. I'd better go before he sees me on my phone and gives me a ticket. See you as soon as I can get there." She said the last in a quick rush of words and then broke the connection.

He tucked the phone away, uneasy for reasons he couldn't put his finger on. The blockade was more intriguing than worrisome, and Honor could hold her own in any situation. He and Ella had been sitting in the shadows of the abandoned building for a couple hours. He hadn't seen or heard a car go by. There'd been no movement at the edges of the lot, no shadows sliding along the pavement where everything should be still. He should feel safer than he had in hours, but his skin was crawling, the hair on his arms standing up. He shifted, pulling out his Glock and checking the chamber. He didn't expect to have to use it again, but he wanted to make sure it was loaded and ready. Just in case.

"Is everything okay?" Ella asked, her voice thick with sleep.

"On the surface, things look great," he responded honestly, because keeping information from her wouldn't help either of them.

"But?"

"That doesn't mean much." He tucked his gun away, scanning the scraggly lot beside the abandoned gas station. There was an old church building beside that—grayish wood-plank siding and boarded-up windows, an old playground in what had probably once been the churchyard. A copse of trees butted up against the back of all three properties and wrapped around the side of the lot he and Ella were sitting in. He eyed the trees, the buildings, the empty lot littered with bits and pieces of people's lives. Bags. Bottles. Papers. Even a shoe.

Nothing moved, but he felt watched.

"I heard you talking about a blockade," Ella said. "Is that something we need to worry about?"

"No." Another honest answer. "One of my coworkers ran into one on the way here. Otherwise, she'd have been here an hour and a half ago. Aside from the holdup, it shouldn't cause us any trouble."

"An hour and a half? How long have we been here? I guess I fell asleep at some point."

"A couple of hours." He scanned the darkness, adrenaline pumping through him. Something was off. He couldn't put his finger on what, but he felt it in the hard quick pulse of his blood.

"That must be some blockade. Are they looking for us?"

"It seems that way."

"Are we looking for something?"

"What?"

"You're watching through the window like you're expecting trouble."

"I'm always expecting trouble, Ella. It comes with the job."

"Good to know. At least one of us is prepared for whatever dangerous thing is about to jump out from behind a tree or a building," she muttered, leaning her forehead against her window and staring out into the darkness.

"I take it your job doesn't put you in these kinds of situations often?"

She snorted. "Often? I'm a non-fiction writer. My job is about as dangerous as buttering a slice of bread. I am woefully unprepared for this."

"If it helps, most people are. And most don't handle themselves as well as you have."

"It doesn't, but thanks for the effort on my behalf."

He'd have laughed at that, but his nerves were humming, his mind shouting that he'd better stay focused. He eyed the empty lot again, then the building they were parked near. The brick facade was spray painted with symbols and words, the ground littered with leaves and trash. His view of the lot on Ella's side of the gas station was blocked by trees. If he were sneaking up on the Chevy, he'd be coming from that direction.

A shadow moved at the corner of the building. Not a person. Just a quick shift from gray to black where nothing had been moving before.

He grabbed Ella's arms, yanking her down forcefully.

The window she'd been leaning on exploded, blunt pieces of glass showering her hair and face, a bullet whizzing by so close to Sam's face he could feel its heat.

He pulled out his gun reflexively. No thought to whether he should. No second-guessing the decision.

"Stay in the truck and stay down until I tell you differently," he commanded as he opened the door and stepped out of the Chevy, the body of the truck between him and the place where the shadow had moved. He saw nothing, but he knew the perp was there, hanging around the corner of the building, trying to get a good shot off without being seen.

"FBI," Sam yelled. "Drop your weapon and come out with your hands up."

"Sure, right. That's what I'm going to do," a man responded, stepping around the side of the building, strutting like a bantam rooster—cocky attitude as clear as the gun he was carrying.

"Put the weapon down and step away from it," Sam commanded.

"No problem." He placed the weapon on the

ground, his gaze darting past Sam to a point just behind him.

Sam whirled around and saw a second gunman stepping around the far side of the building.

Gun in hand.

Aimed straight at Sam's chest.

Sam fired.

The gunman flew back, the gun dropping to the ground and skittering across the pavement.

Sam swung back around, aimed his firearm at the first perp. The guy was edging toward his gun, all his cockiness suddenly gone.

"Move again, and you're dead," Sam said.

"I haven't done a thing to you, man. Let me go, and we'll forget this happened. Neither of has to get hurt."

"The only one in danger of getting hurt is you. On the ground, spread-eagle."

"You wouldn't shoot an unarmed man," the guy responded, gesturing toward the gun that lay a few feet away.

"Try me." But he didn't want to shoot. He wanted to take the guy in for questioning. He might be a low-level member of The Organization, but Sam had no doubt he was on the payroll. "Down on the ground. Now!"

The gunman complied, dropping onto his stomach, his arms and legs spread, fingers splayed, the gun just out of reach of his arms.

He looked like a scrawny kid, his jeans baggy. No jacket. Longish hair. Kid or not, apparently this wasn't the first time he'd been arrested.

"Good choice," Sam said as he stepped around the Chevy.

"Yeah. I make lots of them," the guy muttered, and then he sprang up and took off, racing around the side of the building and out of the line of fire.

FOUR

Ella stayed down.

Just like she'd been told.

Minutes ticked by. Five. Ten. She counted the passing seconds, and she waited. Still. Quiet.

Cold air whipped in through the shattered windows, and she shivered. She could freeze to death before Sam returned, but she still didn't dare raise her head and look around.

Shots had been fired. One that had shattered the window she'd been leaning against. Another that she thought had come from Sam's gun.

She hoped it had.

He could be lying on the pavement, bleeding to death while she sat in the truck. She'd heard him speaking after the second shot was fired. She was certain of that. He'd shouted orders, someone had responded. She'd heard feet slapping against pavement, and then...

Nothing but leaves skittering across the asphalt and wind rushing through the trees. She'd had no idea what had happened, so she'd stayed where she was, but she couldn't stay forever. And if Sam had been hurt, if he needed help and she was sitting around waiting for the next command, she'd never forgive herself.

Clouds had rolled in. She could see them through the broken back window, white-gray against the night sky. The moon was hidden, the night somehow darker, the skittering leaves and rustling trees a reminder that Ella was alone—a sitting duck in an abandoned gas station.

"Sam?" she whispered.

He didn't answer, and she had the horrible feeling that he was gone for good. That he'd run after someone or toward something and gotten injured.

Or worse—killed by someone who was really after Ella.

The Organization?

That's what Sam seemed to think. That, somehow, she'd become the crime ring's target. She'd asked dozens of people hundreds of questions since she'd arrived in Maine, so it was possible he was right. She needed to go to the state police, tell them what had happened and let them deal with things.

Sure, Sam said he was with the FBI and that they were investigating in the area. She'd heard tidbits of his conversations with coworkers, and she could believe he was on the up-and-up, but he was gone, and she was alone, and she couldn't stay put forever.

"Sam?" she tried again. Still no response.

Rain began to fall, splattering against the roof of the truck and dripping in through the open windows.

She eased up. Cautiously. Glanced around.

A man lay on the pavement a hundred yards away. Motionless. Her heart jumped, and she opened the door, was out in the rain running toward him before she realized it wasn't Sam. That the body was too narrow, the clothes wrong.

She stopped a few feet away.

"Hello?" she said. "Are you okay?"

But, of course, she knew he wasn't. Blood stained the pavement around him, the amount so large, she didn't think he could have survived the loss. She felt for a pulse anyway, touching the man's jugular and then his wrist. His skin was already cool.

"I'm sorry," she murmured, wondering if he had a family, wondering how many hearts would be broken because he'd died.

Sorry that he tried to kill you and Sam and wound up dead?

That's what Ruby would have said. She had plenty of compassion for people who wanted to change their lives. She'd devoted her career to fighting drug addiction, to helping men, women and teens who wanted to break their habits and move toward recovery, but she had no patience for people who habitually made bad choices.

People like Ruby's mother.

A drug addict, Andrea McIntire had been more interested in her next high than in her only child. She'd been willing to lie and steal to get what she craved, and she hadn't been at all concerned about making sure her daughter went to school in clean clothes or had food to eat.

Ruby had been in and out of foster care three times before a savvy social worker realized that Andrea had family who might be able to help. By the time Ruby moved in with Rosemary, she was tough, street-smart and impatient. Ella had been eight, still reeling from the deaths of both her parents, living in a giant farmhouse that creaked when it settled at night.

She'd been terrified.

Ruby had been brave.

They'd bonded that first year. Despite the age gap and the vast difference in their backgrounds, they'd connected.

Up until she'd received the news that Ruby had died of a drug overdose, Ella had thought they'd shared everything with one another—secrets, dreams, triumphs, disappointments.

Now, she wasn't sure.

She'd found Ruby's journals at the apartment, and she'd been poring through them. She'd known a lot about her cousin, but she hadn't known that she was a wonderful writer. She hadn't known how easily she understood the nature of the people she worked with. She hadn't known that Ruby felt responsible for every client's relapse, or that she worried about not helping enough.

Ella turned away from the covered body, passing the handgun the deceased must have dropped. She knew nothing about firearms, and she didn't pick it up. She walked back to the Chevy but didn't get inside.

She'd hidden away for long enough.

She wasn't the same terrified kid she'd been after her parents died. She wasn't the wounded and traumatized woman she'd been three years ago. She might not have Ruby's natural toughness, but she knew how to fight and how to survive.

She rounded the vehicle.

A gun lay near the building. Other than that, there was no sign that anyone had been there.

She had a choice—stick around or leave.

She knew what Sam would want her to do, but Sam was gone, and she had no idea if he'd return.

She crossed the empty lot, icy rain sliding

down her head and into the collar of her shirt. She needed to look for help, but having her clothes soaked through on a night this cold was almost as dangerous as sitting in the truck waiting to be killed.

She thought about breaking into the gas station store and waiting there until the rain stopped, but the people who were after her were looking for the truck. They'd found it once. They could find it again. The church seemed like a better option, and she headed there, staying close to the tree line that bordered the abandoned lots. She still felt exposed and vulnerable, every quiet noise making her pulse jump.

She reached the churchyard and darted across it, pounding up the steps that led to the back door of the building. It was locked, the windows on either side boarded up from the inside.

She bounded down the steps again, racing around to the front of the building. Like the back door, the front was locked, the portico that covered it leaning to the side, the rotting roof offering little shelter from the now pouring rain.

There were two windows on the front of the building. Both closed and boarded up from the inside. The glass was intact, but she tried both windows anyway. If she could open them, she might be able to knock down the plywood.

Both were locked. She could break them, but

a broken window would be a neon sign to anyone looking for her.

She rounded the building again, eyeing windows that were just above head level. An old oil tank sat under one of them, rusted but sturdy to the touch. This side of the church faced an empty lot. Beyond that, the gas station stood like an ancient sentinel—old and faded against the landscape.

Her skin crawled, and she climbed onto the tank, the metal giving slightly beneath her weight. She was shoulder level with the window. No barriers beyond the glass. She could see the dark interior of the church, the outline of wooden pews.

"Please let this be open, Lord. Please," she prayed as she touched the cold glass. She pushed upward, felt the window shift. It inched up slowly, stiff from years of being closed. She pushed harder, forcing the swollen window jambs along the frame.

Two inches, three inches. Four.

A sound drifted into her consciousness. Not pattering rain or rustling leaves. A quiet rumble that made her heart jump. A car. Somewhere nearby. She shoved at the window again, frantic to get inside and out of sight.

The rumble grew louder, and she could hear the splash of tires on wet pavement.

Please, Lord. Please.

The window gave a little more, opening almost enough for her to climb through. She glanced over her shoulder, her mouth dry with fear.

A car rounded the corner of the gas station building, moving slowly, its headlights gleaming on wet pavement.

She shoved harder, forcing the window up, shoving her shoulders through the opening. Her jacket caught on something and she slid out of it, falling headfirst onto the church floor.

She lay there. Stunned. Breathless.

Grateful.

A door slammed, and she jumped to her feet, grabbing her jacket and forcing the window closed again. She stood there for a moment. Not moving. Barely breathing. Just listening. Praying. Trying to come up with a plan.

She couldn't stay where she was forever. She knew that.

The rest wasn't as clear.

The faint sound of voices drifted through the window, and she stepped away from the glass, sidling between two pews and stepping into a center aisle. The floor creaked and dust wafted into the air as she walked, tickling her nose and her throat.

The sanctuary was small, the ceiling high,

the church the kind that had been built a century ago—beautiful wood and vaulted ceilings, but no extra space for Sunday school classes or church socials.

If there was an office, it would be near the front of the building. She moved in that direction, shuffling her feet to keep from tripping. The side windows weren't boarded up, but the front and back were, and very little light illuminated the space.

She reached the front of the building and slid her hand along the wall of the vestibule. It brushed across a doorjamb, and she found a knob, was surprised when it turned.

She knew there wouldn't be a phone in the office. If there was one, it wouldn't be functional, but she checked anyway, running her hand over the desk and then a metal file cabinet. The place had been cleaned out. No lamps. No books. Nothing that would help her contact the authorities.

Something thumped against the outside of the building, and she jumped, her heart beating so fast she thought it might fly out of her chest. Had they found her?

She waited, listening.

At first, she heard nothing. Then, another soft thump and the quiet slide of wood against wood as a window opened. She yanked open a desk drawer, searching frantically for scissors, a pencil, anything she could use as a weapon.

She found a pen shoved up against the side of the drawer, and she clutched it in her hand as she moved across the small room and peered out the door.

Icy wind wafted through the vestibule, and she knew a window was open, that someone may have already entered the sanctuary. She eased back into the room, away from the door and the danger beyond it.

There was no place to hide. No escape route.

The window was boarded, and removing the plywood would make too much noise. Her only hope was that whoever was in the church would search the entire sanctuary before finding the office. If he did, she might be able to slip through the darkness and out the window.

It wasn't a good plan.

It wasn't even a decent one, but it was the only one she had.

She waited, listening to the pattering rain and the creak of the building. Whoever had entered the building was moving silently. No footsteps. No rustle of fabric. If she waited too long, he'd find her, so she moved toward the doorway again, stepping out into the vestibule. Feeling like a mouse sticking its nose out of a hole in the wall, waiting for the cat to pounce.

She saw no one, so she eased along the wall, one silent footstep at a time around the corner of the vestibule and into the sanctuary. She could see the open window and the night sky beyond it. She stepped toward it, her view suddenly blocked.

She didn't have time to react or to fight.

Someone grabbed her arm, spun her around. A hand slapped over her mouth and she was pulled against a rock-hard chest.

She kicked backward, her foot connecting with a shin.

Her attacker's grip didn't ease, and she tried the head butt she'd practiced dozens of times after Jarrod had attacked her. The self-defense class had stressed the importance of using the assailant's momentum against him. If that didn't work, a head butt to the chin could loosen his grip.

But this wasn't a class.

The assailant was real, and he seemed to know exactly what she intended. He had her held so closely to his body that she couldn't move her head, his hand so firm on her mouth that she couldn't bite.

She still had the pen, but her arm was pressed so tightly against her side, she couldn't use it.

She wouldn't give up, though.

She wouldn't allow herself to be dragged

away. Or, worse, killed in the church and left there. She slammed backward, her entire body used in the effort, but her assailant didn't flinch, his grip didn't ease, and he was dragging her back toward the vestibule, back toward the office, and there didn't seem to be a thing she could do about it.

Ella was stronger than she looked, her wiry muscles taut as she tried to loosen Sam's hold. He leaned down, his lips close to her ear.

"Calm down," he said, his voice barely a whisper. He'd seen the car pull into the gas station parking lot—a Damariscotta sheriff's cruiser with no lights or sirens on. Just like he'd seen Ella climbing through the church window.

He didn't have time to speculate as to whether the men in the cruiser had seen her.

He'd left the perp bound and gagged in the empty lot next to the garage and he'd headed her way, staying in the shadows as two police officers hopped out of the car and went to the body of the deceased.

Apparently, they hadn't called for backup.

There were no sirens blaring in the background. No flashlights bouncing along the ground.

Wolves in cops' clothing.

That's how Honor had described them, and that's what he thought they were.

Ella stilled, her muscles going slack, all her fight gone.

"Don't say a word, okay?" he continued. "Any questions you have, ask them after we get out of here."

She nodded her understanding, and he took her hand, leading her to the window he'd climbed in. Beyond it, there was nothing but an expanse of overgrown grass that spilled out toward the forest. This must have been the edge of town, once upon a time, the church being the demarcation between the civilized and uncivilized world.

Now it was a place where anything could happen and probably did.

He motioned for Ella to wait and then climbed out the window. She followed quickly, dropping to the ground with a quiet splash. Rain fell in sheets, and that was to their advantage. It would mute the sound of their retreat and make it easier to escape without drawing the enemies' attention.

It would also soak them through and make them colder than they should be.

Ella was already shivering.

He didn't mention it, and she didn't complain. The woods were a hundred yards ahead, and he wanted to reach them before the phony officers decided to search the church property.

He took Ella's hand, moving quickly and quietly, his heart thudding a quick, even rhythm. This wasn't the first dangerous situation he'd been in, but it was the first time he'd had an innocent civilian with him while he tried to escape notice.

He could hear men's voices and the swish of feet in wet grass. Close.

Ella must have heard the same. Her muscles tensed, but she kept moving, heading away from the church and toward the trees. They ducked under the canopy of a huge maple tree as the two men walked around the side of the church. Casually. Easily. As if they had all the time in the world to find their victims.

They sure didn't seem to be in any hurry to help the guy Sam had tied up and left behind.

Nor did they seem interested in calling for someone to retrieve the body of their fallen comrade.

But then, this was a multitiered crime ring.

He doubted they knew or cared about either of the hired gunmen. Their goal, their mission was to find and stop Sam and Ella.

Sam's goal and mission was to keep that from happening.

He led Ella deeper into the woods, the fragrant scent of pine needles and fall rain swirling around them. The highway was due west of the gas station. He was certain of that, and he glanced through the trees. The moon wasn't visible, and he couldn't use it to navigate, but he could hear the quiet rumble of traffic somewhere in the distance.

He aimed for that, pushing through forest growth, so thick he thought it had been decades since anyone had walked there.

He was tempted to take out his phone and call Honor, but he was afraid the glowing screen would be spotted through the woods and make them an easy target for a sniper's bullet. The first two gunmen had been terrible shots. He couldn't count on the second two being the same.

Ella stayed silent as they navigated the hushed woods, her footsteps muffled by a thick carpet of pine needles and dead leaves.

He'd told her to stay in the Chevy.

She hadn't.

It may have saved her life.

He'd been herding his captive back to the gas station when he'd spotted her at the church, standing on an old oil tank, trying to open a window. Seconds later, the police car had appeared. He had no idea if they'd seen her. He'd been too busy tying up the gunman to notice anything but the way his heart was racing, his adrenaline pumping. He'd had to use his utility knife to cut strips of the perp's jacket and use those as bonds, and it had all taken way too long.

She'd been inside the church by the time he finished.

The fake cops had been looking in the Chevy.

If she'd been there, things could have gone really bad really fast. He was a good shot, but he didn't know if he could have taken down both men before they'd had a chance to kill her. He was glad he hadn't had to try. Her choice to go inside the church hadn't been a good one, but he couldn't fault her for trying to find a place to hide.

They were moving uphill, the tree growth sparser, and he could feel the rain again, falling on his head and neck in icy sheets. He glanced at Ella. Her hair was hanging in her face, sticking to her cheeks and the column of her throat. Rivulets of water streamed from her temple to her chin and dripped onto her shirt. She didn't try to brush the water away. She seemed focused on moving forward, her jacket hanging open, the hood lying lank against her back.

"Hold on," he said, pulling her to a stop.

"And let them catch up? I'd rather not."

"They're probably still back at the church."

"You really think so?" she asked, glancing over her shoulder as if she expected the two men to appear.

"I don't know, but I doubt they're going to want to hike through the woods in the pouring rain."

"That depends on how much they stand to lose if you and I get away."

She was right about that, and he wasn't going to argue.

"You're right, but we have a second, and that's all this will take." He zipped her jacket, pulled up her hood and tugged her soaked hair beneath it. "There. Done. Let's go."

"You do know that I'm capable of zipping my own coat and pulling up my hood, right?" she asked, as they started walking again.

"I'm confident that you're capable of whatever you set your mind to, but your mind was on other things. Like getting out of these woods and finding a way to safety."

"Is your friend anywhere nearby?" she asked, her teeth chattering on the last word.

"I figure a glowing phone would be a perfect beacon in a dark forest, so I haven't texted or called her." They reached the crest of the hill, and the highway was a hundred feet below, cars and trucks flying past, rain dancing in glowing headlights.

It was the best thing he'd seen in a few weeks, and if he'd been alone, he'd have navigated the steep grade that led down to it. He wasn't sure if Ella could manage, though. She seemed fit and coordinated, but she was also cold. That could make movements clumsy and muscles weak.

"Come on." He took her arm, his hand cupped around her bicep as he walked along the edge of the precipice. There'd be an area where the grade was less steep, the descent less treacherous. Once he found it, they'd head down and he'd call Honor.

"In case you haven't noticed," she said, her breath a cloud of white fog, "the road is right there."

She pointed, her entire arm shaking.

"And climbing down with frozen fingers and toes will be difficult," he replied. "So we're going to find an easier path."

"If we don't get shot before then?"

"We're not going to be shot."

"You want to know something, Sam?"

"Sure," he responded, eager to keep her talking and focused. She was colder than anyone should be, her body trembling almost violently. He pulled her close, wrapping his arm around her shoulders, trying to share some of his warmth.

She tensed but didn't protest and didn't move away.

Obviously, she felt as cold as she looked.

"You were going to tell me something?" he prodded, and she shrugged.

"Nothing important. I was just thinking that if anyone had asked me two weeks ago, I'd have told them that my cousin wasn't going to die, that I wasn't going to drive to Maine and that I wasn't going to be kidnapped while I was there. But here we are, and all those things have happened. Maybe being shot before this is over isn't so far-fetched."

"Maybe getting down to the road, getting in a vehicle and getting out of this alive isn't, either," he responded.

"And getting back to Charlotte where it's warm," she added.

"Charlotte, North Carolina?"

"Yes."

"I thought I heard some Southern charm in your voice."

"Yours is pretty thick with it, too."

"I'm originally from Houston. I moved to Boston a few years ago."

"To work at the FBI field office there?"

"Yes."

"So who were you before you·became Special Agent Sam Sheridan?"

"A Houston police officer."

"Law enforcement all the way?"

"It was that or become a criminal." It was the truth, but he expected her to laugh like most people did when he made the comment.

She didn't, and he met her eyes, realized she was watching him through the darkness.

"I get that," she said.

"Do you?"

"Sure. My cousin had the same choice to make. Do good or do harm. Her mother was a drug addict. Ruby decided to be the opposite. She got her PhD in counseling, had a master's in social work and devoted her life to helping people fight their addictions."

"She sounds like a great person."

"She is. Was," she corrected herself quickly.

"Was she originally from Charlotte, too?"

"Chicago. Until she moved in with me and my grandmother when she was thirteen."

"What brought her to Newcastle?"

"A job. She worked at the medical clinic. That's why I was there. I wanted to clean out her office, but the door was locked."

His pulse jumped at her words, his mind shooting in a dozen directions it hadn't gone before. "You mentioned she was a social worker at the Damariscotta Medical Center, right?"

"Yes. She was employed by the county, but Damariscotta is the largest medical center in the area, so they set her up in an office there. She did a lot of things. Most of it involved working with recovering drug addicts, their kids and family."

"That's interesting."

"Is it?"

"Yes," he responded, the word almost drowned out by the sound of something or someone crashing through the woods.

"What is that?" Ella whispered.

"I'm not sure."

"I know you're out here!" a woman called. "I'm tracking you on my phone."

"They've found us!" Ella hissed, and then she took off, scrambling down the steep incline toward the road below.

FIVE

She made it halfway down before she slipped, her feet losing traction in the loose wet soil. She grabbed for something. Anything. A rock. A branch. One of the scraggly bushes that jutted out from the face of the rocky hill.

She found a hand. Warm. Calloused. Familiar.

Sam. Of course.

He dragged her back up the hillside without a word, navigating the path with an ease she envied.

"We need to get out of here," she panted as they reached the top. Terrified. Desperate. Ready to run, and not sure why he wasn't.

"I agree," a woman intoned, stepping out from between towering pine trees. She was staring down at a phone, the glow of the screen painting her face with greenish light. She appeared to be young. Maybe twenty-three or four, her hair cut in a pixie style that framed her narrow face. She was waiflike—but with a gun peeking out from beneath her coat.

"I was beginning to think you'd given up," Sam said as she approached.

The woman tucked the phone away and shrugged. "Sometimes it takes me a while to achieve a goal, but, generally speaking, I never give up." She strode forward, offering Ella a firm handshake. "I'm Special Agent Honor Remington."

"Ella McIntire."

"Nice to meet you, Ella. Seeing as how you're freezing, I'll give you my coat."

"That's not necessary," she said as Honor took her phone from the pocket and shrugged out of the duster.

"You can continue to freeze if you want, but I'm layered up, so I won't be cold if you take this." She handed the coat to Ella and glanced at her phone. "The tracker worked better than I'd hoped, Sam. I followed the signal from the highway and it brought me straight to you."

"I hadn't realized you'd put one in my phone," Sam said.

"I thought I mentioned it before you left for Newcastle."

"You didn't."

"Hmmm. I meant to. The tracking goes both ways. You punch this icon here—" she jabbed her phone screen "—tap the name of the person you want to find and there you are!"

She turned the screen so Ella and Sam could see a small pulsing red arrow and a glowing green one.

"I don't think I have that icon on my phone," Sam said, and Honor nodded.

"Right. Because if someone got nosy and looked at your phone, we wouldn't want them wondering why you want to track someone named Honor. I'll show you how to access the program once we get back to my place."

"Is that where we're headed?" he asked, taking the coat from Ella's hands and urging her into it.

"That's where Wren and Radley are going to meet us. Unless you have a better plan."

"I'd like to go to Ruby's apartment," Ella said.

"That's not a good idea," Sam responded.

"I don't see why it's not," she responded, even though she did. Even though she knew that going back to the apartment would be the expected thing, the thing that the men who'd kidnapped her would be waiting for.

"I don't see why we're standing around in the cold rain discussing this when we could be in my nice warm SUV," Honor cut in. "Come on. Let's get out of here."

She obviously expected them to comply.

She started walking quickly, moving parallel to the road, her gaze fixed on the highway below. How she kept from tripping over a rock or root, Ella didn't know, but she managed it.

Ella wasn't as confident. She'd nearly fallen down the steep hill once; she didn't plan to repeat the mistake.

"There she is!" Honor crowed, gesturing toward a vehicle sitting on the side of the road, its flashers on.

"How did you manage to get from down there to up here?" Ella asked, eyeing the steep descent that was between them and the vehicle.

"It's not as precarious as it seems. Just follow me." She started down, picking her way sideways across the rocky terrain like she'd been born to do it.

"Let's go," Sam said, taking Ella's arm and urging her to follow.

"Is there another option?" She'd never been a fan of heights. She preferred farmland to mountains. Valleys to peaks. She liked to hike through forest and follow trails along rivers, but climbing rocks or scaling cliffs appealed to her about as much as having a root canal did.

"Not currently," he replied. "But I think Honor is right. This isn't as steep as it looks."

"Right," she muttered, looking straight down. Way down. Probably eighty to a hundred feet.

A truck whizzed by, spraying water onto the narrow shoulder. If she fell, she'd either break her neck or be run over by an eighteen-wheeler.

"You're not afraid of heights, are you?" Sam asked.

"Not when I'm standing on the ground looking up at them."

"Okay. So you are." He touched her cheek, looked straight into her eyes.

She should have moved away.

She knew that, but she stayed right where she was, looking into eyes that were probably blue or green, the lighter colored irises surrounded by a darker ring.

He was a handsome man.

She'd noticed that in a perfunctory way.

Now she was noticing it more.

"Unfortunately, we're up here," he said. "The SUV is down there. We've got to get down. It's not that high, and getting to the bottom isn't going to be nearly as difficult as it looks."

"I'll tell myself that as I'm plunging to my death."

He chuckled. "Don't worry. I won't let you fall."

She wanted to tell him that she wasn't his responsibility. That she didn't need him to hold on to her arm or to keep her from falling. That all she really needed was a ride back to Ruby's apartment. She could manage things from there. Call the state police, collect the things she planned to bring back to Charlotte and get out of town.

"Tell me more about your cousin," he said, his hand wrapped around hers as he headed down the hill.

"What do you want to know?" she replied, her mouth dry, her focus on the ground, the rocks, the traffic speeding by below.

"How long had she been in Newcastle?"

"Three years."

"And she worked at the clinic the entire time?"

"Yes. She'd been working in Charlotte, but she was looking for a change. She found the job posting on the county website and applied. They asked her to come for an interview. A month later, she was packing up and moving."

"Was she happy with that decision?"

"Yes." She frowned, remembering the journals and Ruby's beautiful loopy handwriting.

"You don't sound convinced."

"I am. I was."

"But?"

"As long as I've known her, Ruby has journaled. She has dozens of notebooks filled with her thoughts in the attic of the farmhouse where we grew up. I've never read them, but I found a bunch more at the apartment."

"You read those?" he asked.

"Yes." She'd had to. She'd wanted to know the details of Ruby's life, and she'd wanted to know what had led to her death.

Not drug addiction.

She couldn't believe that.

Or wouldn't.

"Was there something in them that made you think she was unhappy?"

"Not really, but she mentioned being worried about a few of the people she worked with."

"Worried that they'd hurt her? Or worried in general?"

"Worried in general. Which seemed out of character for her. Ruby was never the kind of person to waste time worrying about things that might not happen." Ella, on the other hand, worried plenty. She thought it might have begun after the car accident that killed her parents. Her grandmother had said she'd always been prone to it. *A trait from your mother's family. Just like your beautiful hair and your gorgeous eyes*, she'd always said.

Maybe she'd been right.

All Ella knew was that Ruby had been the confident cousin. She'd been the timid one. They'd both matured, grown and changed, but those general tendencies had remained the same. Ruby had faced life with gusto and excitement. Ella eased into every new situation with a little trepidation and a lot of caution.

"Did she say what she was worried about? Specifically, I mean?"

"One of the people she was helping had missed a couple of group sessions, and she wrote that she didn't understand why. He'd seemed eager to kick his habits and make a fresh start, and she'd lined him up with a job." She shrugged, remembering the words and the jotted number in the margin of the page. A phone number, maybe. She hadn't called it.

"I'd think that wouldn't be all that unusual. Relapse is more the norm than the exception when it comes to drug addiction."

"I know. Ruby did, too. She spent her life watching people make progress, fall backward and then pull themselves back up again."

"She spent her life offering a hand to help them do it," he said. "That had to be exhausting and disheartening at times."

"She didn't kill herself, if that's what you're implying." The words popped out before she could stop them. "Forget I said that."

"Why?"

"Because I know you weren't implying anything."

"You're right. I wasn't, but now I'm curious. Did the police tell you that she killed herself?"

"They implied it was a possibility."

"Why?"

"You ask a lot of questions, Sam."

"Someone kidnapped you, Ella. I don't think you need to be reminded of what could have happened."

"I didn't believe what the coroner listed as cause of death," she said, because Sam was right. She could have been killed out in the woods, and there wouldn't have been one person out looking for her. "I went to the police and told them that. They explained that I was wrong to question the findings."

"What were the findings?"

"Ruby died of an opioid overdose. They said if it hadn't been accidental, she'd done it on purpose, and then they'd asked me if she'd seemed depressed prior to her death."

"I see."

"I doubt it. Ruby was never depressed. She loved life. She loved her job. She loved her friends and her church family. There's no way she killed herself, but she couldn't have overdosed, either. Her childhood was ruined by her mother's addiction. She was terrified of becoming like her. I think I saw her take an aspirin once while we were growing up—that's how adamant she was that drugs were bad for the body and mind. There's no way she became an addict. None."

"So you came here to clean out her apartment and to find out the truth?"

"Something like that."

She expected him to tell her that she'd wasted her time, to explain all the reasons why the medical examiner and coroner were right. She expected him to do exactly what the police had—tell her that she should pack up her cousin's life and go back home. Move on. Hold on to the memories. Let go of the sorrow.

"Okay," he said instead.

"Okay what?"

"We've made it down in one piece, and on the way, I learned some valuable information," he responded.

He was right.

They were almost at the bottom of the hill.

Surprised, she took the last few steps down to the shoulder of the road. "I guess you were right. It wasn't as difficult as it looked."

"Most things aren't," he responded, offering a quick smile.

"Are you two coming?" Honor called, already at the SUV and standing near the driver's door, staring at her phone. "Looks like Wren and Radley are twelve miles from my apartment.

ETA twenty minutes. If we hurry, we should be there around the same time."

She closed the hood and hopped into the vehicle, turning on the engine before they arrived.

"Is she always so energetic?" Ella asked as Sam opened the back door for her.

"Unless she's working on something computer-related," he responded. "Then she's dead still and half deaf. Buckle up."

He closed the door and pulled out his phone, walking a few feet away.

"I feel like I told him I was in a hurry," Honor said, but she didn't seem bothered by the delay. She didn't seem all that curious about the phone call, either.

Ella was.

If Honor hadn't been sitting in the car with her, she might have been tempted to roll down the window and listen in.

As it was, all she could do was pull her seat belt across her lap and wait for his return.

The drive to Honor's apartment was quick and uneventful. Twenty minutes of highway. Five minutes of winding through the backstreets of Newcastle. The houses were small there—the kind Sam imagined fishing families had lived in during the '50s. Now, they were mostly rentals, a few For Sale signs sitting squarely in the center of postage-stamp-sized lots.

Honor's apartment was in a newer section, close to the tourist areas. The building was three stories of balconies that overlooked the Damariscotta River.

"Don't get too excited," she said, as she pulled into the attached parking garage. "I don't have a river view."

"I'll try to contain my disappointment," Sam said, scanning the cars as she drove through the first level of the garage and up to the second. The area was dimly lit, the parking spots mostly full. There was a vehicle gate that had to be accessed with a pass, but anyone could walk in without a problem. If he'd wanted to harm someone who lived in the apartment, he didn't think it would be difficult to do. Duck under the gate. Hide between a couple of cars. Wait.

"Don't worry. There are security cameras everywhere, and they're monitored 24/7," Honor said as if she'd read his mind.

"That doesn't mean a whole lot," he responded.

"Maybe not, but if we're killed, there'll be a record of it."

"That's…comforting," Ella murmured.

She'd been silent during the drive, and he hadn't pressed her to speak. She'd given him enough information to start investigating. He had her cousin's name, occupation and cause of death. He knew where she'd worked and who her employer was.

He knew she was dead and that Ella didn't believe it was an accident.

She also didn't believe it was suicide.

That only left one other option.

Ella hadn't mentioned murder, but he knew she'd been thinking it. She'd come to Newcastle to find out the truth. He had to assume she'd asked a lot of questions, pushed a lot of buttons, gotten a lot of people's attention.

One of them wanted to silence her.

Maybe more than one.

Ruby had been a social worker. He'd assume she had access to background information on all the people she worked with. He'd also assume she worked with adults and teenagers. Some from good homes. Some in foster care. Some who were transients or runaways or simply living off the grid.

According to Bo, those were the people The Organization preyed on.

Disconnected. Unloved. Homeless.

He frowned, tapping his fingers against his thigh, impatient and restless. He preferred action to idleness, and this assignment had meant a whole lot of sitting and a whole lot of doing nothing.

Until now.

Now things had heated up.

Yeah. His cover had been blown, but he still thought they were a step closer to shutting down the Newcastle cell. He'd called Wren as soon as he'd reached Honor's vehicle and asked her to do a quick background check on Ruby McIntire. She said she'd have the information before she arrived at the apartment.

He was anxious to see what she'd come up with.

If Ella was right, her cousin had been murdered.

But she could be wrong.

Love often made people see things that weren't there. Loyalty where there was none. Compassion where only apathy existed. It wasn't a stretch to think that someone could miss signs of depression or addiction if she wanted to.

And for three years, the two women had lived a thousand miles apart. Had they visited each other frequently? Talked regularly? Had the relationship changed after Ruby moved?

"Here we are," Honor said cheerfully as she pulled into a numbered parking spot on the second floor of the garage. "Home sweet home. Until I can get back to my real home with my real bed and my real job." She opened the door and hopped out.

If he hadn't known her so well, Sam would have thought she wasn't paying attention to her surroundings, looking for trouble, focusing her energy on making certain everything was exactly the way it should be.

He knew her methods, though. She might seem distracted and unaware, but Honor was all about details. If a chair in the office was moved, she'd notice. She read her surroundings the way other people read emotions in people's faces. She collected the data like a computer, spinning it through her mind at breakneck speed.

"Looks good," she said, and he opened Ella's door and pulled her out.

"No lollygagging, folks," Honor continued, leading the way to a door in the cement wall. "It might look good, but things can change on a dime, and they usually do."

She unlocked the door, stepping aside so Ella could step in first.

"Apartment 230, Sam. Here's the key. I was outside the least amount of time, so I should be the one to do reconnaissance. I'm not expecting to find anyone lurking around near the front door of the building, but if I do, I'll let you know." She was gone before he could respond, jogging through the gloomy garage, heading for the stairwell that would take her to the lower level of the garage.

"I thought we were all going to the apartment together," Ella said uneasily.

He stepped into the carpeted hallway, closing the door before he responded. "We are."

"And, yet, she's out there, and we're in here."

"You heard what she said. She'll be up once she makes sure the area is clear. And it should be. As far as we know, The Organization has no idea she exists." He touched her shoulder, steering her down the hall.

She went, but her muscles were tense, her movements tightly controlled.

"Is there some reason why you don't want to be in the apartment alone with me?" he asked, keeping his tone conversational and light.

"Who said I wasn't comfortable?"

"Your tension. Your facial expression. Just about everything except your words." They reached apartment 230, and he wasn't surprised to see a colorful wreath hanging from the knocker. Fall leaves and plastic gourds were attached to a foam ring. Handmade, he was certain. It looked like one of Honor's creations.

"We're strangers," Ella said, her gaze focused on the wreath, as if staring at it would somehow solve whatever problem she was having.

"Not quite. I know your name. You know mine. I know you're afraid of heights. You know I've been working undercover."

"Right," she murmured, her arms folded across her stomach, Honor's coat bunching under them.

She looked vulnerable and scared, and he'd have stood there trying to figure out why if he hadn't been worried about being seen. No one in The Organization knew Honor, but Sam had a feeling most of them knew him. His name. His face. If he was seen by someone who had that information, his whereabouts would be reported to whomever was calling the shots. It wouldn't be long before an army of assassins showed up to take him out and drag Ella away.

He unlocked the door and gestured for her to enter.

She did so reluctantly.

She didn't have to say anything for him to know that.

"Relax," he said, hanging the keys on a hook near the front door. "I'm not going to turn into a werewolf when the moon is full."

"That's what they all say," she replied, offering a smile that didn't reach her eyes.

Gray eyes, he noted.

Unusual and pretty, her lashes light brown and thick.

She was shivering with cold, or fear, her skin leached of color, her fingernails tinged with blue.

"You've had a lot of werewolf boyfriends?"

he asked, grabbing a throw from the back of a recliner and tossing it around her shoulders.

"Just one. That was enough," she said it lightly, but there was nothing light about the look in her eyes. He'd seen it before—terror mixed with confusion and, often, relief that it was over. That the abuse had been survived.

"Who was he?" he asked, keeping his tone as light as hers had been. His skin felt tight, though, his blood boiling. He'd learned to control his rage a long time ago, but it could still simmer over if he let it. He didn't let it. Ever. It was too easy to hurt someone in the heat of the moment. With words. With fists. Easy to hurt, but not so easy to heal.

"No one I want to talk about."

"I respect that, but someone kidnapped you, Ella. Do you think he had anything to do with that?"

"No."

"Could he have had anything to do with what happened to Ruby?"

"No."

"You're certain?" he pressed, and she frowned, using the edge of the throw to wipe away water that was dripping from her hair to her forehead.

"As certain as I can be. He's in jail. Apparently, being tossed in prison for a couple of months didn't cure him of the need to use his fists when he didn't get his way. His second fiancée was in the hospital for three weeks. He got a seven-year prison term for that."

"Second fiancée? I take it you were the first?"

"I said I didn't want to talk about it."

"You said you didn't want to talk about *him*," he corrected, and she smiled. A real smile that spread across her face and gleamed in her eyes.

"You're playing word games with a writer, Sam."

"No games," he responded. "Being in prison doesn't always keep someone from seeking revenge. Do you think he has a grudge against you?"

"I testified on behalf of the prosecution at his second trial, so he might, but he was incarcerated two years ago, and I don't think he has any idea that Ruby moved up here. If he were going to send someone after me, he'd send them to my house in Charlotte. I live alone and work from home. He knows that."

"We'll check into it anyway."

"And then what?" she asked, walking across the room and reaching for the curtains that covered a sliding glass door.

"Don't," he said, and her hand fell away.

She didn't turn around, though, just stood with her back to him, her head up, her shoulders straight. "Once you realize that he had nothing to do with this, are you going to keep trying to find out what happened to Ruby?"

"Yes."

"Because you think her death is connected to The Organization?"

"Partially."

"What's the other part?" She swung around, the hood covering her hair, layers of clothing and blanket shrouding her body. She'd looked vulnerable before. She still did, but she also looked tough and determined.

She wouldn't give up on finding the truth about her cousin.

She'd do it with him, or she'd do it on her own.

"Your cousin deserves justice, and I plan on making sure she gets it."

A key scraped in the lock, and the door opened.

Honor walked in, Wren Santino and Radley Tumberg right behind her.

"We're here. Finally. The rain slowed things down," Wren announced, her gaze moving from Sam to Ella. "Ella, I'm Wren Santino. Sam and I work together." She didn't mention that she was Sam's supervisor and the head of the Special Crimes Unit.

But that was Wren—confident, humble. As willing to serve as to be served. She worked as hard as anyone on the team did, and she never asked anyone to do something she wouldn't. When a case was solved, she spread credit over the entire team, refusing to accept accolades from her higher-ups.

"Nice to meet you," Ella said, taking the hand Wren offered.

"It would be nicer if it were under better circumstances. Sam told me about your cousin's death. I'd like to extend my deepest condolences." She spoke with sincerity, her dark eyes filled with compassion and understanding. This was one of the things Wren did best—offering empathy and understanding to victims of horrendous crimes, extending sympathy to those who'd suffered losses, saying just the right words at just the right time in exactly the right way. Sam liked to watch her in action, and he'd tried to emulate her methods, but whatever she had was organic. It couldn't be faked or copied.

"Thank you," Ella said, visibly relaxing.

"This," Wren continued, gesturing to Radley, "is Special Agent Radley Tumberg. I've put him in charge of gathering evidence regarding Ruby's death. We'll keep you updated on the results. Currently, we've received the coroner's report and the police report."

"That was fast," Ella said, and Wren smiled.

"Having FBI tacked at the end of your title

can really help get things moving. It looks like you're soaked through and half frozen. Why don't you take a hot shower and warm up? We'll discuss things when you're not so cold."

"I'm fine."

"You're not, but you will be," Wren said, dropping a messenger bag and a computer case on the sofa. "Where's your bathroom, Honor?"

"Just down the hall and to the right."

"Why don't you show Ella? Maybe set her up with some dry clothes? You're close to the same size. I'm sure you can find something that fits her."

"I've got just the thing," Honor said, hooking her arm around Ella's waist and leading her to a wide hallway. "I've been taking a knitting class. Just to keep busy when I'm not working. I just finished a gorgeous sweater. Charcoal gray and cream."

"That sounds…nice," Ella responded, her gaze flitting from Honor to Sam. "Are you all going to still be here when I get back?"

"Where would we go?" he asked, and she shrugged.

"To Ruby's apartment? To the medical center? To your place?"

"For now, we're staying put," he replied.

"Okay. Good."

"Come on. You're not getting any warmer standing around in those wet clothes," Honor said, urging her away.

Sam watched them go, surprised by his response to Ella's question, to the quick, strong need to reassure her.

Obviously, he was more tired than he felt.

He raked a hand through his damp hair. "I wonder if Honor has a coffee maker around here?" he said.

"Probably," Wren responded. She'd dropped onto the sofa and had her laptop open, but she was watching him intently.

"What?" he asked.

"You and Ella seem to have bonded over your experience."

"Yeah. That's what happens when you're with someone while you're being shot at," he said.

She didn't respond. She didn't look away.

Like always, she had her hair pulled back into a neat bun, her suit tailored impeccably. There wasn't a speck of lint or a bead of water on the fabric.

"You've been in combat, Wren. You know what I'm talking about."

"Yes. I do."

"Then why do I feel like you have something you'd like to say about it?"

"When has she ever not said something that was on her mind?" Radley cut in. Tall and lean, he had blond hair, blue eyes and the kind of good looks women seemed to notice.

If he cared about that, he didn't let on.

In the few years they'd worked together, he and Sam had become friends. They'd camped together a handful of times, gone hunting the previous fall and spent a couple Sunday afternoons watching football together.

"You have a point," Sam said, walking into the galley-style kitchen. There was a coffee maker on the counter. Old school and inexpensive.

"He usually does, so how about we move on?" Wren typed something into her laptop. "Start the coffee, and then take a look at this."

"What?" He pulled a package of coffee filters and a container of coffee grounds from a cupboard.

"The police report for Ella's cousin. The sheriff was sent the electronic file, and he told me I wasn't going to find anything noteworthy in it."

"Did you?" He started the coffee and took a seat beside her on the sofa. Radley pulled the recliner over and leaned in, his elbows propped on his knees, his hands lax. He'd probably already heard whatever Wren had to say, but he was the kind of agent who liked to look at evidence and information from dozens of different angles.

"Did Ella mention that Ruby was found in her car?"

"No."

"She bought it last year."

"Is that important?"

"Not really. Just a little side note. The police didn't bother conducting any interviews after her body was found, but they did process the scene. They found a book, a half-eaten sandwich sitting on a piece of paper towel on the passenger seat." She jabbed toward the computer screen, and he saw the photos she'd pulled up.

Pristine car.

The sandwich on the seat. A few crumbs scattered across black leather. A book lay on the console, open and face down.

"Her body was discovered by her supervisor. He noticed her car still parked in its normal spot across the street from the clinic when he arrived for work. He didn't think anything of it until she didn't show up for a scheduled meeting. He walked across the street, looked in the car and found her there. He called the police."

"Looks like she was died during her lunch break the previous day?"

"Apparently, she often ate lunch there when it was too cold to eat outside."

"Was it cold that day?"

"Very, and when the police arrived, the gas tank of her car was empty and the keys were in the ignition. It seemed to them that she'd had the car on when she'd decided to shoot up."

She scrolled to another image—a woman slumped over in her seat, a tourniquet around her arm, a needle lying on her leg. She'd fallen against the door and had probably been hidden from the view of anyone passing by.

"That seems convenient," he said, and Wren nodded.

"I was thinking the same. I was also thinking how strange it is that she took a few bites of the sandwich before she shot up. Addicts don't like to wait."

"There wasn't a struggle," he pointed out. "No visible bruises. No sign that she tried to fight."

"True, but I found something interesting in the blood toxicology report." She scrolled through several pages of documents and stopped. "She had high carbon monoxide levels in her blood."

"How high?"

"High enough to kill her." She met his eyes.

"The only reason why the coroner called the death a result of drug overdose is that she had lethal amounts of opioids in her blood, too."

"The police didn't feel the need to investigate the carbon monoxide poisoning?"

"They did. She'd backed her car into the space, and her muffler was close to a cement wall. They speculated that CO was leaking into her car. When she overdosed, the car kept running and she kept breathing in carbon monoxide until she died."

"How feasible do you think that is?"

"About as feasible as me fitting into the petite sizes at the clothing store. I can try, but it's never going to work."

"So, Ella was right. Someone murdered her cousin."

"It looks that way. Here's what I think. Ruby made a habit of eating lunch in her car. On chilly days, she turned the engine on. Anything that's a habit can be observed. The day she died, the temperature was in the high fifties with lots of cloud cover."

"Sounds like you're done your research," Sam said.

"Don't I always?" She raised a raven-black brow and continued, "Someone wanted Ruby dead. Whoever it was knew about her rituals and habits. He or she waited for a chilly day, blocked the muffler with something and sat back and watched. Ruby got in her car, started the engine to warm herself up. Started eating lunch. Maybe felt sleepy. Passed out. The killer opened the door, set the stage and shot her up with enough drugs to kill ten people."

"Overkill?"

"Based on what I've read in the report, I'd say so." She closed the computer and met his eyes. "What do you think? Reasonable theory?"

"More than reasonable." He could picture it going down—the dreary cold day, Ruby escaping the busy medical clinic and sitting in her car, engine running, good book in hand.

She would have had no idea what was happening to her, no way of knowing that she was about to die. Her life had been snuffed out without fanfare, her death made to look like it had resulted from the thing she'd been fighting against her entire adult life.

If not for Ella, then Ruby would have been labeled a secret drug addict and probably forgotten by the community and the people she'd served.

That's the way her murderer intended things.

It wasn't the way things would play out.

Sam was confident of that.

They knew the way Ruby had died. They

knew the weapons that had been used. Now all they had to was find a motive, find the perpetrator and make him pay.

SIX

Ella fell asleep to the sound of voices drifting into Honor's guest room. She'd been brought there after her shower, given a bottle of cold water, a cup of herbal tea and instructions to get some rest.

She'd had a feeling Sam and his coworkers wanted to discuss things without her around. She could have refused to stay in the room, but she'd needed some time to clear her head.

She'd told Sam about Jarrod.

Not in so many words, but in enough words that she knew he'd understood. Aside from Ruby and the police officers who'd responded to her 911 call, she'd never shared that information with anyone.

It was too difficult.

Too embarrassing.

Too painful.

She'd told one of her therapists that and been assured that the way she felt was normal. It didn't feel normal. Nothing about her relationship with Jarrod had.

But that was water under the bridge, far enough in the past that it only hurt when she thought about it too much. And she'd told herself she wasn't going to think about it. Not while Sam and his coworkers were in the living room discussing her kidnapping and Ruby's death and The Organization they were trying to shut down.

She'd lain in bed and listened to the rhythmic pulse of four people's voices, and she'd found herself comforted by them, by the presence of people who'd been strangers a few hours ago.

She'd fallen asleep thinking about that, and she'd woken to sunlight streaming in through the cracks in the blinds and someone tapping on her door.

"You up?" Honor called, her voice as cheerful and filled with life as it had been the previous night.

"Yes," she said, pushing aside the blankets and rushing out of bed.

"I put some fresh clothes in the bathroom. Go ahead and shower. Wren wants to head over to your cousin's apartment in twenty minutes. Can you be ready?"

"Sure."

"Great. The guys are gone. They're grabbing some breakfast. I'm afraid my pantry isn't stocked for five people. They should be back shortly."

"All right," Ella said, opening the door and looking into Honor's gamine face. She looked wide-awake and well rested despite her late night. "Thanks for all your help, Honor."

"No problem. Sam and Radley went back to the clinic last night. They found this in the security office." She held up Ella purse.

"I must have dropped it when I was kidnapped."

"Did they take anything from it?"

Ella rifled through the oversize bag. Her wallet was there. Her credit cards. Sixty dollars in cash and her bank card. All of it present and accounted for. Her keys were there, too, still attached to the lanyard. Her cell phone was tucked into the side pocket. She had a small copy of the New Testament in another pocket, and that hadn't been touched. Mascara. Lipstick. Compact. Everything exactly where it usually was. "It doesn't look like it."

"That's what we figured. More than likely, your kidnappers didn't realize you'd dropped it."

"What about my car?" she asked. She'd left a box of Ruby's things behind the front seat of the station wagon. Her cousin's laptop and day planner were in it.

"No sign of it. They probably hot-wired it and hoped that if you and your car disappeared at the same time, no one would ask questions. Fortunately, you're still around." She smiled. "I hate to chat and run, but I've got a class to teach at the community college. I'll be back this evening. See you then."

"Sounds good," Ella said, but Honor was already halfway down the hall.

Wren was probably somewhere in that direction, but Ella didn't want to waste time looking for her. When the men returned, she wanted to be dressed and ready to go.

She hurried into the bathroom, took a quick shower and dressed in the clothes Honor had provided—a soft cable knit sweater dress that fell to her knees, the royal purple deep and rich. Thick lavender tights. Chunky boots that were a size too big. There were toiletries in a small basket Honor had left near the clothes, and Ella brushed her hair, then pulled it back into a ponytail.

She didn't spend too long looking in the mirror.

The circles under eyes had been getting deeper since Ruby's death. Her skin had the sallow pallor of someone who never went outside. She was a hot mess, and she shouldn't care.

She *didn't* care.

And yet, she had the absurd urge to brush on some mascara, powder her nose and apply lipstick.

The front door opened, and she could hear the men's voices, Wren's voice mixing with them. She was as ready as she'd ever be, so she opened the door and stepped into the hall.

Sam was there.

Just a few feet away.

Thick blond hair. Bright blue eyes. A face that could have graced the cover of any magazine. But she'd never been swayed by looks. She'd never dreamed of marrying the best-looking guy in college or the most attractive man at church.

The heart was what mattered.

She'd known that before Jarrod.

She still knew it.

And Sam's heart?

It seemed as beautiful as dandelion seeds drifting in a sunlit meadow.

"You're awake," he said, smiling in a way that made her heart jump and her knees go weak.

"So are you."

"I guess we both have keen observational skills," he deadpanned, and she laughed.

She couldn't stop herself.

Sam smiled in response, his gaze dropping from her eyes to her mouth and back again.

Her laughter died and her pulse jumped.

She thought he knew it.

He brushed a strand of hair from her cheek, his callused fingers rasping against her skin. "Don't stop on my account," he murmured.

"Stop what?"

"Laughing. They say it's good for the soul." His hand dropped away, and he stepped back. "There are coffee and doughnuts in the kitchen. Juice in the fridge."

"I'm fine."

"You might not feel that way in a couple of hours when your stomach is growling and Radley has eaten everything in the apartment."

"I thought we'd be in Ruby's apartment soon. I bought eggs and milk and cheese a couple of days ago. We can bring them back here. If I'm hungry by then, I'll make an omelet."

"*We're* not going to be anywhere, Ella. You'll be here. I'll be at your cousin's place," he said.

"When was this decided?" she demanded.

"A few minutes ago."

"Why wasn't I included in the discussion?"

"Because you don't work with the Special Crimes Unit. You're a civilian. We have an obligation to keep you safe."

"I don't see how I'd be any safer here with one FBI agent than I would be at Ruby's with two," she said.

"She has a point," Wren called from the living room, her voice crisp and precise.

Sam scowled.

"She's right. I do," Ella said, stepping past him and walking into the living room. Wren and Radley were both sitting on the couch, doughnuts in hand, coffee cups on the table in front of them. "What time are we leaving?"

"Any time you're ready," Wren replied, taking a last bite of doughnut and standing up. She brushed a few crumbs from her pant leg and emerald-colored shirt. Then pulled on her jacket.

"I'm ready," she said.

"Honor gave you the purse and keys?"

"They're here." She held up the bag.

Sam was right behind her. She could feel his presence like a physical touch, and she glanced over her shoulder.

She wasn't sure what she expected. Maybe a hint of censure in his eyes. Clenched fists. Tension in his jaw or mouth.

She knew the subtle signs of anger.

She'd seen them dozens of times when she was with Jarrod.

Sam didn't look angry. He didn't even look frustrated. He looked relaxed, rested, ready for whatever the day brought.

"We can grab your cousin's journals while

we're there," he said, conceding defeat without an argument. "Maybe there's something in them that you missed. If you don't mind, we can read through them, too. Several sets of eyes are better than one."

"Okay," she said, pushing aside guilt and the sickening feeling that she was betraying Ruby. The only real betrayal would be in allowing her death to stay classified as a drug overdose.

"She wouldn't hold it against you," he said quietly, and her throat went tight with tears that she didn't want to shed. Not in front of Sam and his coworkers.

"I know," she managed to respond, turning away from his sympathy, because seeing it only made her feel more like crying.

"Are you ready, Radley?" Wren asked, grabbing her coffee and taking a sip. "If Ella is going, you may as well come along, too."

"Way to make a guy feel needed," Radley said, plucking a second doughnut from a box that sat on the kitchen counter and smiling in Ella's direction.

He had a nice smile.

A nice face.

Nice eyes.

And, as far as she'd been able to tell in the short time since they'd met, he was a nice person.

"Trust me, your skill set will definitely be

needed today," Wren responded, grabbing her phone from the coffee table and dropping it in her jacket pocket. "If we're going, now is as good a time as any. We'll go to Ruby's place and then make a pit stop at the medical clinic."

Ella's pulse jumped, and she found herself glancing at Sam, meeting his eyes. They weren't nice. Not like Radley's. They were beautiful, sharp, stunning. As clear a blue as she'd ever seen, rimmed with dark teal.

"You didn't mention the clinic when we discussed our plans this morning," he said, his gaze never leaving Ella's face.

"I didn't realize Radley would be with us," Wren replied. "I want access to Ruby's office and to the server room you've been working in. More than likely, anything important has already been removed, but I want to look. Even the most careful criminals make mistakes. It's possible something was left behind that can be used to shut them down."

"We could ask for access," Radley suggested, setting the box down and pulling out his wallet. "Or, we could get a search warrant. That *is* what most law enforcement officers would do."

"I've already put in the request for the search warrant, and it'll be in my hands before we reach the clinic, but we've been down this road before. Places like this are notorious for losing keys and taking hours to find them," Wren replied. "If that's the way things play out, you can do what you do best and pick the locks."

"What I do best," he commented, pulling several credit cards from his wallet and looking at each one, then sliding one in the back pocket of his jeans, "is hit a moving target at twelve-hundred yards, but if you need a lock picked, I'm your man." He grabbed a coat from a closet near the door and put it on, then walked into the hall, Wren following close behind him.

"Hit a moving target at twelve-hundred yards?" Ella repeated, running that through her mind—how far that was and how difficult it would be.

"He was a marine sniper," Sam offered, as he grabbed his coat, looked through the closet and took another. He held it up, eyeing it critically. "Is this a dark gray peacoat?"

"Yes."

"Then it's the one Honor told me to give you." He handed it to her, waiting as she shrugged into it.

When she finished, he straightened the collar, his knuckles brushing the side of her neck and the underside of her jaw. Just light quick touches. Not intentional. She knew that, but she felt them in the pit of her stomach and in the dark little spot in her heart that she'd closed off years ago. The one she'd once filled with love, hope and expectation.

She moved away, her pulse thrumming rapidly. She wanted to call it fear. That would be the easy answer.

But she knew it was something different— that first quick flutter of attraction, that deep longing to move closer, to look more intently. To study, learn and understand.

To connect in a way that wasn't light, friendly and comfortable.

She shoved the thought away.

No way did she plan to forge a deep connection. Not with someone like Sam. He was cut from different cloth than other men she'd known. Not the standard dress-suit variety of fabric, he was faded flannel made of worsted yarn. Soft cotton. Scratchy wool. Raw silk and tightly knit alpaca.

Natural.

Unpretentious.

Intriguing.

And, if she allowed it, irresistible.

She wouldn't, because she was happy with her life, with her comfortable house and her quiet existence. She liked the silence of being alone, the ease of only having herself to answer to.

She liked being safe from heartbreak and pain.

And she liked Sam.

The last thought popped in her head unbidden. Unwanted. Undeniable.

"We'd better get out of here," she murmured, avoiding his eyes as she darted for the door and out into the hallway.

The drive to Ruby's place wasn't silent.

Most commutes weren't when Sam was with team members.

They spent the travel time discussing cases and working through strategies, because time was a commodity none of them liked to waste.

Wren had handpicked every member of the unit, bringing in men and women who had skill sets she thought would be helpful in pursuing justice for the most vulnerable citizens. Children. Women. The elderly. They were the people the Special Crimes Unit served most frequently, the victims it had been created to help.

The Special Crimes Unit took cold cases and new ones. They tracked down murderers, rapists, kidnappers and pedophiles. They tossed criminals in jail, comforted victims and spent every day trying to do more to make the world a safer place.

A few months ago, the team had taken down the Night Stalker, a prolific serial killer who'd been targeting young ER nurses. The streets of

New England were safer because of it, but Sam and his coworkers hadn't spent much time celebrating the victory.

Success always felt sweet.

Failure was never an option.

And predators were always waiting for a chance to pounce.

Which meant the clock never stopped ticking, time never stopped mattering. An overlooked clue or unprocessed piece of evidence could mean a criminal remained free, so commutes were spent discussing case details and going over evidence. Once. Twice. Dozens of times.

This commute wasn't any different. Wren was explaining that Special Agent Adam Whitfield had arrived in town four hours ago. He'd gone to Bo's house, but the informant and his family were gone. Adam had reached him by phone, and he'd said Bo had been cagey and nervous. He'd offered no new information regarding the way The Organization's Newcastle cell operated, and he'd told Adam that as far as he was concerned, he was out of the entire mess.

He refused to give his location, but when Adam asked if he'd known Ruby, Bo had been willing to answer. He and his wife had been in a drug rehabilitation class she'd taught. They'd both liked and respected her, and they'd both been shocked when they'd learned that she'd died of a drug overdose.

As far as Bo knew, Ruby hadn't been on The Organization's payroll, but he'd told Adam that there were plenty of people walking around town who were probably secret members of the crime syndicate. If she'd been able to hide a drug addiction, Ruby could have hidden her affiliation with The Organization.

Sam glanced at Ella as Wren made the pronouncement.

She was staring out her window, silent and tense.

"It's an angle we needed to check into," he said, and she nodded, her glossy ponytail sliding across her shoulders and falling straight to the middle of her narrow back.

"I know."

"What are your thoughts, Ella?" Wren asked as she turned the corner onto a picturesque street—dark lampposts with old-fashioned streetlights, large trees still covered with colorful leaves. Large Victorian houses set in the middle of oversize yards.

A Norman Rockwell painting waiting to happen.

"Ruby didn't lie. She didn't cheat. She didn't

take advantage of people. She was honest to a fault, and I can't imagine her ever agreeing to take part in any of the things The Organization does."

"Sometimes," Sam said gently, "love doesn't give us clear vision."

"And sometimes it does," she replied, still staring out the window.

"Turn left here," she said as they rolled toward a four-way stop. "Ruby's apartment is in the last house on the street. She had a great view of the river."

He could see that—the Damariscotta River sparkling in the watery sunlight, a few boats scattered along its surface.

Wren pulled into the driveway of a three-story building that had been built in the early 1900s. It had been a house back then, the beautiful red maple in the front yard probably planted by the original owners.

Now, the house had been portioned into apartments, the driveway widened to accommodate eight cars. It was empty now, a few leaves skittering across the cement as Wren parked.

"Looks like the other renters are out," Radley commented as he opened his door and stepped down.

"The other four tenants are doctors or nurses who work at the clinic," Ella offered. "They leave early and get home late. Ruby described them all in one of her journal entries. I guess they're all single like she was. No spouses, significant others or kids. I've been in town for almost a week, and there's never been anyone here during the day."

"Then if I find someone hanging around, I'll know he or she doesn't belong. Give me five minutes to check the perimeter." Radley closed the door and disappeared around the side of the house.

He'd been a sniper with the marines and served two tours in Iraq. He believed in caution and in quick action.

Sam admired those traits.

He *possessed* those traits.

Everyone in the unit did.

Wren stepped out of the car, and he knew she was studying the house across the street and the one next door, looking at the yards and the shrubbery, the places where someone might hide.

She had her left hand in the pocket of her dark slacks, the fabric of her tailored coat pulling back to reveal a crisp white shirt and her shoulder holster. She looked like what she was—a professional, a federal officer, a woman who knew how to take charge and how to step back.

"I feel redundant," Ella said.

"Once we're in the apartment, you won't," he responded.

"Maybe not. How much time can we spend there?"

"Probably not as much as you'd like."

"I need a week's worth of time. I've boxed a lot of Ruby's things, but I still have the desk in her room to go through, and she had a lot of clothes. I should probably donate them." The sadness in her voice was unmistakable, and he touched her arm, waited until she looked at him.

"I'm sorry this is happening to you, Ella."

"Things could be worse," she responded.

"That doesn't make it better."

"I guess it doesn't," she responded.

She hadn't slept well. That was obvious. She had dark circles under her eyes and deep hollows beneath her cheekbones, but her skin was smooth, her nose and cheeks dotted with freckles that made him think of hot summer days and long lazy summer nights.

There was something about Ella that tugged at his heart in a way few things had. It wasn't her vulnerability. It sure wasn't the situation she found herself in. He'd worked with plenty of victims, spending time interviewing them, protecting them, reassuring them. None of them had made him wonder what it would be like to walk into their open arms at the end of a long day.

Maybe it was just her. The straight approach she took to things. Her loyalty to her cousin. Her willingness to leave everything she knew to find out the truth.

He opened his door, taking Ella's hand and tugging her across the seats and out his side of the vehicle.

SEVEN

The front door to the house was already open, Radley standing beside it, back to the building as he watched the street. He'd have noticed anything unusual and neutralized any threat, but Sam still headed for the house at a brisk jog, his hand wrapped around Ella's.

She kept up easily.

Which was good. The less time they spent in the open, the happier Sam would be.

It took seconds to reach the door and step across the threshold. Each one felt like a private invitation to a sniper's bullet.

He pulled Ella inside and far enough away from the door that she couldn't be seen from the street.

Or shot from it.

"We made it," Ella said as if she'd thought they wouldn't.

"Maybe a little too easily," Wren replied, staring up a wide stairway centered in the middle of a huge foyer. "I'm trying not to let that worry me. This place is immense, by the way."

"It was the biggest building in town for a half a century. Built by a shipping magnate right around the end of the nineteenth century. He had sixteen kids, and he wanted each to have his or her own room. That wasn't something done at the time, but it sure made it easy for the current owner to convert the place to apartments," Ella said, pulling her keys out of her purse and heading up the stairs.

"You know a lot about the property," Wren commented, but Sam doubted her mind was on the conversation. As she'd said, the house was huge. Lots of doors. Lots of alcoves. Lots of places for someone to hide.

"Ruby told me that story a dozen times. I think the idea of a family that big and a father who cared that much fascinated her. Her apartment is on the second floor," Ella responded, the words a little rushed and a little breathless.

She was nervous or scared, but she was trying not to show it—moving up the stairs quickly.

She stopped on the second-floor landing, pointing up the stairs that led to the next floor. "The third level is being converted to a penthouse apartment. Ruby was thinking about making a rental offer on it once it was complete."

She led them across the gleaming hardwood

floor, passing a small reading nook near an oval-shaped stained glass window.

Two doors opened off the oversize landing. One white. One orange.

Ella hurried to the brightly colored one. "This is it."

She unlocked the door, and probably would have stepped inside, but Sam tugged her back.

"Let Wren and Radley go in first."

"You don't really think someone would hang around in the apartment waiting for me, do you?" she asked, but she didn't try to follow.

"It isn't about what I think," he replied. "It's about keeping you safe. That requires taking precautions. Have you met your cousin's neighbor?" he asked, gesturing at the other door.

She shook her head. "He's a doctor, though. Ruby wrote about him."

"What'd she say?" Usually victims were murdered by loved ones or acquaintances—people who knew their routines and their habits.

"That he had a big mouth and cocky attitude, and she was glad that their offices at the clinic were two floors apart."

"Interesting."

"Why?"

"Most victims know their murderers."

"So you think she *was* murdered?"

"Don't you?"

"Yes, but you're the first law enforcement official I've spoken to who agrees."

"Wren was able to get copies of the police and coroner's reports. We went over them last night."

"And?"

He hesitated, not sure if he should tell her what they suspected—that Ruby's muffler had been purposely blocked, that she'd been knocked out by carbon monoxide poisoning before she was injected with opioids.

"I can handle whatever it is. So if that's what you're worried about, don't," Ella prodded, a hint of impatience in her voice.

"Who said I was worried?"

"Come on, Sam," she said, ignoring the question. "Spill. It's not like I'm going to melt into a puddle of fresh grief if you tell me how Ruby was killed. Besides, she was my family, and I think I have a right to know."

She was my family.

Not: *She was family.*

There was a big difference in the words and the meaning, and he was sure Ella had intended him to notice. Without Ruby, Ella was family-less. No siblings. Both parents dead in a car accident years ago. No surviving aunts, uncles or grandparents.

Sam knew the facts. He'd seen them printed

in black and white the previous night. Wren was thorough, and she hadn't missed a thing. Not even the police report Ella had signed against her ex-fiancé. The one that had contained photos of her bloodied face, her bruised arms, X-rays of her broken ribs.

She'd pressed charges against her ex, and Sam had read a transcript of the trial that had come from that.

Yeah. He knew a lot about Ella, but he didn't know how she'd react when he told her how her cousin had died.

He explained anyway, outlining the theory Wren had presented the previous night.

When he finished, she offered a quick, curt nod.

"Thank you."

"I'm—"

"Please don't say you're sorry again, Sam."

"Convinced Ruby knew her killer," he continued. "That's why I'm interested in her neighbors."

"Right. You can read more about them in her journals. She wrote about all the people in her world."

"Including you?"

"Probably. I didn't read the earlier ones. I was mostly skimming the recent one, trying to find a reason for what happened."

"Did you find information about any significant relationships?"

"Romantic?"

"Yes. And friendships. Did she write about anyone in particular?"

"She mentioned her boyfriend a lot. Ian works at the medical clinic. He's a doctor there."

"Do you have a last name?"

"Wade. I met with him the day I arrived in town. He seemed heartbroken by Ruby's death." She mentioned the last casually, as if Ian Wade's reaction to Ruby's death didn't matter.

But, of course, it did.

Maybe Wade's sorrow was real. Maybe it wasn't. Either way, Sam made a mental note to speak with the guy.

Boyfriends, fiancés, husbands and exes were always the first in a list of suspects.

"Were they serious?" he asked, and she shrugged.

"As serious as Ruby ever was with any guy."

"That's an interesting way to put it."

"Ruby was an interesting person. She loved her job. She loved life, but she preferred not to fall in love with anyone. At least, that's the way she always explained it to me."

"So she had more than one boyfriend at a time?" Someone like that could have a list of spurned lovers interested in seeking revenge.

"No. She kept her relationships light. No deep feelings or high expectations."

"She was a cynic?"

"She was the opposite of that. She believed in love and happy endings and good people. She just didn't want to be part of a couple. She enjoyed her independence too much."

"I wonder how Ian felt about that?" he asked, and she shrugged again.

"Ruby was always clear on the parameters of her relationships before she entered them. The last thing she ever wanted to do was hurt someone."

That didn't mean she hadn't managed it.

And hurt feelings could result in festering resentment. He'd worked in law enforcement long enough to have seen many examples of how that could manifest itself.

He'd definitely be speaking with the doctor soon.

Fabric rustled, the sound of boots on floorboards drifting from the apartment. Seconds later, Radley appeared in the open doorway. "It's all clear. Come on in."

Ella went immediately, rushing into the apartment.

Sam followed, stepping into an immaculate living room.

Dark wood floors that were probably original.

Huge fireplace with a carved mantel.

Large window with a view of the river.

The curtains were open, sunlight falling on a built-in window seat covered with blue velvet fabric. There were built-in bookshelves on the far wall, an old secretary desk nestled in an alcove they created it.

"Wow," he said.

"I was thinking the same thing," Radley murmured. "Who'd mind coming home to this every night?"

"Ruby loved it. When I walked in for the first time, I understood why she'd gushed about living here. It's every bit as beautiful as she said."

"How often did you visit?" Sam asked.

"Never." There was finality in the word and regret. "I had a lot of excuses. None of them should have kept me away."

"Regrets will eat you alive if you let them, Ella," he said.

"If knowing that would keep them at bay, I'd spend my nights sleeping peacefully instead of chasing a bunch of what-ifs." She smiled, the expression bittersweet. "Ruby knew I loved her, and she visited me a few times a year, so it's not like we hadn't seen each other recently. I still wish I would have made the time to come here while she was alive and seen it through her eyes."

"Her journals have probably helped you do that," Radley cut in.

"Not really. She wasn't big on writing about inanimate things. She preferred to focus on people. There are a couple of descriptions of the place, but mostly just because she was speculating on what it might have been like before it was converted to apartments. Hold on. I'll show you what I mean." She stepped around an oversize couch, moving toward inset bookshelves that ran from flooring to ceiling. Stopped.

The color leached from her face, and she crouched, touching an empty bottom shelf. "They're gone."

"What?" he asked, but he was pretty sure he knew.

"The journals."

"Are you sure?" It was a stupid question, and he knew it. Ella had spent nearly a week in the apartment. She'd read the journals, and she knew exactly where they should be.

"Yes. They were here when I left the apartment yesterday morning."

"Did you mention the journals to anyone other than me?" Sam asked, and she nodded.

"I went to the police, assuming that they'd see what I had—Ruby's concern, her anxiety, the subtle hints that something was wrong. They copied a few of the pages I pointed out but said they didn't see anything concerning. The sheriff told me to come back if I found enough evidence to reopen her case. So I reread the journals a dozen times."

"And didn't find anything else alarming?"

"It was alarming to me. Like I've said, Ruby's last few journals had a different tone than her previous ones. She mentioned the clinic a lot and some of the people she worked with. She also jotted a few numbers in the margins of the most recent. I've been trying to figure out what they mean, because I didn't want to go back to the police unless I was certain they could act on the information."

"Did you take photos of the pages?"

"No, but I was reading through it again yesterday morning. I put it in the bottom drawer of the secretary desk, and…" She straightened hurrying to the old desk. The scuffed wood had been polished to a high sheen and a place mat sat on the opened desk, a computer mouse next to it.

It looked like Ruby's computer had been there.

If so, it was gone. Just like the journals.

Ella knelt in front to the desk and wrestled with the bottom drawer. He leaned down to help, brushing her hands away and giving a quick, sharp tug.

It popped open.

He saw the journal before she removed it.

Dark brown leather. Slim. Dates scrawled across the top in silver calligraphy letters.

"It's here," Ella said, lifting it and opening the pages.

The writing inside was as beautiful as what he'd seen on the cover.

"What's going on?" Wren asked, stepping into the room from the wide hallway that Sam assumed led to the bedrooms.

"Most of the journals are missing," he said, and she frowned, pulling out her cell phone and dialing quickly.

"Anything else gone?" she asked.

"I don't know," Ella responded. "Ruby liked to hold on to anything related to people she cared about or good memories she had. She packed a lot into this apartment."

"How about we go through room by room?" Sam suggested.

"All right." She tucked the notebook in her purse and led him through a tall archway and into the kitchen. Unlike the living room, it had a modern feel. Granite counters. Deep porcelain sink. White cabinets.

The counters were bare, several taped boxes sitting on a sturdy farmhouse table. Ella touched one as she passed.

"I packed four. There are four here. That's pretty much it for dining and kitchen stuff. Ruby was a wonderful person, but she was a horrible cook. She ate a lot of carryout."

She walked to an exterior door that was set against the corner of the wall at the back of the room.

"This is unlocked. I'm sure I locked it before I left the house. I'm a little OCD about that kind of stuff."

"Where does it lead?" Sam asked, motioning for Radley to check the lock on the small window above the sink. It was too small for most people to crawl through, but someone Ella's size could manage it. If The Organization was responsible for the missing journals, they had plenty of members who could probably do it.

"A balcony that overlooks the river. The fire escape is attached, so it serves dual purposes."

"Have you used the balcony since you arrived?" Sam asked, checking the jamb near the lock, looking for signs that someone had forced his or her way in.

"Yes. Once or twice. But, like I said, I'm OCD about locks."

"It's a skeleton lock," Sam commented. "Do you have the key?"

"Sure. It's hanging…" She touched a small nail on the wall near the door. "It was here.

Now it's gone. Ruby's purse is gone, too. It was there." She pointed to an ornate silver hook. "I haven't touched it since the day I arrived."

"Was it something she used every day?" Sam asked, surprised that it would have been left behind when Ruby went to work.

"Yes, but she didn't leave it here, if that's what you're thinking. It was found in her car. The police gave it to me when I arrived. Her wallet was in it. Credit cards. Normal things."

"Cell phone?" he asked, his mind jumping back to the police report. He'd skimmed the list of items found in the car. He didn't recall a cell phone being listed.

"No. It wasn't in the purse or in her car. I thought it might be in her office, but you know how my attempt to look for it ended."

"I don't know anyone who carries a cell phone and leaves it when they go out." Radley tucked his hand in his sleeve and turned the door handle.

"The police are on the way," Wren said, entering the kitchen and looking around. "What have we figured out so far?"

"Whoever broke in probably came in this door. It's two floors up but easily accessible if you have a ladder, and these old skeleton locks are a cinch to pick," Radley responded. "I'm curious to see if the fire escape has been accessed."

He pulled on the doorknob.

The door remained closed.

"You have to push it. It swings out," Ella said, and he turned the handle again, pushed. It still didn't open.

"Is it stuck?" Ella asked. But it obviously was, and Sam wanted to know why.

"Seems that way," Radley said calmly, but Sam could see his tension and hear the edge in his voice. "I'll go outside and look at it from the street. Maybe I can figure out what's going—"

A shrill alarm drowned out the rest of his words.

A siren shrieking a warning.

Loud. Insistent.

"Fire alarm!" Wren shouted above the din, grabbing Ella's hand and dragging her from the room.

Sam sprinted ahead of them, heading for the apartment door on Radley's heels. They reached it simultaneously, and Sam slid his hand across the wood.

"Cool," he shouted, pulling his gun and yanking the door open.

He was expecting gunfire and dove to the side to avoid it, but the landing was empty.

No gunman. No sign of trouble. Nothing but the shrieking siren and the thundering pulse of his blood.

Radley tapped his shoulder, motioned that they should split up. One up to the third floor. One to the lower level.

He nodded his agreement, gun still out as he moved toward the neighbor's door.

He tried the knob. Found it locked. Moved toward the stairs. And smelled smoke, the scent acrid and pungent, chemical and rancid. Tendrils of black snaked through the floorboards and drifted upward, swirling in the hazy sunlight that streamed through the window. He could feel heat through the soles of his shoes and knew the fire was burning hot below, feeding on the dried-out, century-old joists and beams.

He ran to the stairs, could see the front door—flames lapping up from the floor, eating away at the wood, the heat curling the paper on the nearby wall.

The bottom of the stairs was in flames as well, the railing alive with orangish fire.

Blocked fire exit.

Blocked front door.

Blocked escape.

A well-thought-out plan, but it wasn't going to be successful.

Sam spun around, lifting the edge of his shirt to cover his nose and mouth as he ran back into the apartment.

EIGHT

The day had gone from calm to chaos so quickly Ella's head was spinning.

Or maybe it was the smoke that was making it do that.

Wren had tugged her into the hallway, while Sam and Radley ran out of the apartment. Within seconds, black smoke had seeped up through the floorboards, filling her lungs and stinging her eyes.

The siren stopped screaming, the sound dying abruptly, and the silence was more terrifying than the cacophony of noise had been.

"What happened?" she said, her throat raw, her voice hoarse.

"The electricity must have shorted out the alarm. It should be running on batteries, too, but sometimes landlords get lazy," Wren replied, dragging Ella a few more feet down the hall.

The bathroom was there, and she must have known it.

She opened the door and shoved Ella into the room.

"Turn on the faucet. Wet some towels. Quickly."

Ella did as she asked, grabbing a pile of towels from the linen closet and tossing it into the claw-foot tub. She ran water over them, coughing as smoke billowed into the room.

"Good enough. Let's go," Wren shouted, grabbing the towels and tossing one around Ella's shoulders.

"Wrap it around your head. Cover your nose and mouth."

They stepped back into the hall, and the smoke was so thick, Ella could barely see.

"Let's get low and get out," Wren shouted, yanking Ella to the floor, the sound of flames crackling and wood splitting almost drowning out her voice.

That was worse—much, *much* worse—than the sound of the siren had been.

"What about Sam and Radley?" she tried to shout, but the words caught in her throat, and she coughed so violently she saw stars.

The floor seemed to be burning from beneath, the wood warping as she crawled back toward the kitchen. She knew Wren was ahead of her, but she could barely see her through the thick smoke.

Please, Lord, she prayed. *Get us all out of here alive.*

Her knees and palms burned, but she managed to find her way through the hall and into the kitchen. The smoke was lighter there—a misty gray cloud that floated through the room.

"We need to get the door open," Wren shouted, dragging Ella to her feet and pulling her to the balcony door.

The emergency exit.

The one that was blocked.

"The window will be quicker," Ella responded, the back of her throat tasting like ash and hot coal, her eyes streaming with tears she didn't have time to wipe away.

Her purse was still over her shoulder, the towel wrapped around the lower part of her face as she ran to the sink and fumbled with the window's lock.

Her fingers were clumsy, but she finally managed it, shoving it open so that cold air blew in. Somewhere deep inside the house, the fire roared.

She could almost picture it.

Growing bigger. Feeding off the old wood and the dry wallpaper, the pretty couches and lovely throw rugs.

"You think you can get through there?" Wren

asked, suddenly at her side, the lower part of her face covered, the upper part smudged with soot.

"Easily." But she suddenly realized that Wren probably could not. She was tall and willowy, but her shoulders were broad. Even if she *could* manage to squeeze through, there was no way Sam and Radley could.

Sam.

She'd been trying not to think about him fighting his way through smoke and flames, trying not to think about how it would feel if he didn't make it out. If she was the reason that he died.

Because this was her fault.

If she hadn't been asking questions, if she hadn't been so determined to find the truth, she would have already finished clearing Ruby's apartment and would be back in Charlotte by now, and Sam would be still be working undercover. Doing a dangerous job, but safer than he was right now.

"Ella!" Wren shouted, shaking her arm. "Did you hear what I said? Get out that window. Now!"

"Let's try the door instead," she responded, dodging around Wren and grabbing the door handle. She slammed her shoulder against the door, but it wouldn't budge.

Someone grabbed her arm, and she whirled around.

"Stop trying to call the shots and help me with this," she shouted, her voice hoarse.

Only it wasn't Wren. It was Sam. Standing right in front of her, a wet towel draped around his shoulders, his hair black with soot.

She wanted to throw her arms around him, tell him how relieved she was that he was okay, but he was dragging her back to the sink while Radley and Wren worked on opening the door.

She could barely hear the rhythmic thump of their shoulders hitting the door. She could barely see them, either. The smoke had become thicker, the room dusky with it. Light filtered in the window, tiny bits of debris floating on the chilly breeze.

"Climb out and head down the fire escape. If that's not functional, dangle and drop. You might break a leg, but you'll be alive."

She didn't move.

She didn't want to die, but she couldn't imagine living, knowing that she'd saved herself while three other people perished.

"Do you need help?" Sam asked, as if her exiting through the window was a foregone conclusion.

"I'm not leaving without you," she responded. *Without* all *of you* was what she'd meant to say.

There was no time to correct the mistake.

Flames jumped through the floor near the kitchen doorway, crawling up the wood trim, and suddenly, she was in Sam's arms, floating through thick smoke and sooty air.

Up and over the sink, feetfirst out the window.

No warning. No chance to argue.

She was in the kitchen and then she was out, cold air bathing her hot skin as she stumbled backward and fell against the sturdy railing.

There were flames to her left, crawling up the wood siding of the house. Flames below, shooting out the windows.

Flames everywhere except the bright red balcony and the chair that stood beneath it, back beneath the knob, legs pressed up against the bottom of the door.

She yanked it away, and the door flew open, Wren and Radley tumbling out, their eyes wide with shock.

Sam came next, grabbing her hand as he ran past, leading her to the side of the balcony farthest from the flames.

"Good job, Ella," he said, his voice so hoarse she could barely understand the words. "Now let's get down from here before the whole house implodes. Where's the fire escape?"

She pointed to the far railing, and the metal

staircase that descended from it. Flames were shooting out from the wall, wrapping the metal with serpentine fingers.

"That's a no go," Wren said, suddenly beside them. "We'll have to go down over the hard way. Quickly, because I think this thing is ready to fall."

"I'm down," Radley said, climbing over the railing and lowering himself so he could grab the cement floor. "Lower her to me once I reach the ground."

He dropped, landing on his feet with fluid grace. "Lower her down! We're running out of time," he shouted.

"Your turn, Ella," Sam said, and she realized that she was the person Radley had been referring to.

She didn't argue.

She didn't want to waste time.

Her heart pounded frantically, and she was shaking as she climbed over the side, her fingers tight around the railing.

"It's going to be okay," Sam assured her. "I'll lower you down as far as I can. Radley will catch you as you fall."

He dropped onto his belly, sliding his arms through the slates in the railing.

"Give me your hands," he said, and she unfisted her right hand, stretched down to grab his warm palm.

"That's it," he encouraged. "Now the other one."

"Hurry!" Radley yelled, and Ella knew they were running out of time.

She grabbed Sam's other hand, closed her eyes and let herself fall off the edge of the balcony.

Ella dangled ten feet above the ground.

Not far, and with Radley ready to break her fall, Sam felt confident she wouldn't be hurt, but she was clutching his hands in a death grip, her eyes closed as she swayed in the open air.

She was light enough that he could have held her there for hours, but the balcony shook, and he knew they only had seconds to escape.

"Ready?" he yelled over the roar of the fire.

She opened her eyes and looked up at him, the terror in her face unmistakable.

"Yes," she said, and he knew it was a lie. She wasn't ready to fall ten feet.

Not many people were, but he wasn't ready to die, and he wasn't ready to do it knowing that she was dying, too.

"Good. Ease your grip, and I'll let go."

"Right." One heartbeat of hesitation and her fingers went lax.

He let her go, clambering over the railing as she dropped.

Radley caught her easily, hands around her waist as he lowered her to the ground. Then, he pulled her out of the way, dragging her toward a private dock that jutted out onto the river, far away from the flames and the gutted house.

That was his cue to go, and he glanced at Wren, saw that she'd climbed over the railing, too.

She nodded once, then dropped down, grabbing the cement floor of the balcony and lowering herself over.

Sam followed, dropping to the ground quickly, the sound of sirens and shouting voices carrying over the roar of the fire.

The house trembled, one of the balconies giving way and crashing to the ground.

"Let's get out of here before falling debris does what the fire didn't," Wren said, jogging toward the river.

Sam followed more slowly.

Someone had set that fire.

Sam had smelled the chemical accelerant mixed with the scent of burning wood and electrical wires. He hadn't smelled it when he'd walked in. He was sure Wren and Radley hadn't, either.

They would have retreated if they had.

So someone had entered the house after them, poured the accelerant out near the front door, on the stairs and—based on how quickly the structure had been consumed—probably in half a dozen other places. If Ella hadn't been able to squeeze through the window, and if she hadn't found a way to open the door, they'd all be dead.

Two birds with one stone—plus a couple of unintended victims.

It would have been a good day for The Organization.

Now, it was going to be a bad one.

Sam pulled out his cell phone and dialed Adam Whitfield's number, waiting impatiently for him to pick up.

He did on the fifth ring. "Hello?"

"We've run into some trouble. Has Wren contacted you yet?"

"She didn't have to. I was going to rendezvous with the four of you after I met with the local PD. I was on my way when I saw smoke. I figured you were in the thick of it. Is everyone okay?"

"Yes, but the apartment we were searching is gone."

"You do know that apartments don't just disappear, right?"

"Gone, as in up in flames. The entire building is going to collapse."

"I'm assuming faulty wires didn't cause the fire."

"You're assuming right."

"What do you need me to do?" He cut to the chase, just like he always did. That was one of the things Sam liked about him. He didn't waste time, didn't hesitate.

"Everyone who lived in the apartment building worked for the clinic."

"That's convenient."

"Yeah. Very. Did Wren fill you in on what we were looking for there?"

"Some journals that might have information about Ruby McIntire. She thinks there's a connection between her death and The Organization."

"I do, too. I also think it's interesting that so many clinic employees are living in the same building. It's not close to the center of town. No way to walk to work or even to bike."

"Friends hooking friends up with places to stay?" he suggested.

"Maybe, but when I moved here, The Organization set me up in an apartment next door to the clinic. They sent the address, a key and information about how and where to pay rent."

"So you think that's how three medical professionals ended up renting apartments in a building that just went up in flames?"

"Four. If you count Ruby."

"Wren doesn't believe she was involved with the syndicate."

"I don't, either, but I think her death is, and I think there might have been a good reason someone wanted her to rent that particular apartment."

"What reason?"

"She was a social worker. She led classes for recovering addicts, so she had plenty of contact with people who were disconnected from society and from family."

"The perfect victims if you're into human trafficking. Grab someone who won't be missed, who will never be searched for, and you don't have to worry about getting caught."

"Right," Sam agreed.

"So what do you want me to do?"

"Find out who owns the property. Individual or corporation. Check for ownership of the building my apartment was in, too. If they're the same, we may have a good lead to pursue."

"Got it. Anything else?"

"Yeah. Check with the state police. We're looking for a car with North Carolina tags registered to—"

"Ella McIntire?"

"Right."

"How long has it been missing?"

"Twenty-four hours. Maybe a little longer."

"Got it. I'll be in touch." He ended the call, and Sam walked across the field of scraggly weeds that separated a lush yard from the river and the dock.

He could see Wren, phone pressed to her ear. Radley was beside her, hands in his pockets, gaze on the crowd of gawkers that had formed a few hundred yards away.

Ella was sitting, her feet dangling over the water.

"Sam!" she shouted, her voice still hoarse, her face stained with layers of soot. She didn't wait for him to step onto the dock. She jumped up, rushing toward him and throwing her arms around his waist.

He was surprised.

Pleased.

Touched.

"You're okay!" she said. "I was worried you'd been hurt when you jumped."

"It wasn't that far to the ground," he said, smoothing loose tendrils of hair from her cheeks, not caring that Radley and Wren were watching.

"It sure felt like it to me." She glanced past

him, her hands brushing against his sides as her arms fell away.

He wanted to step close again, pull her back into his arms, but she was looking at the house, watching as the flames consumed what remained of it. "Everything is gone," she said quietly.

"Not everything. We're still here."

She met his eyes and smiled. "True. And I've still got my purse. No need to get new ID or bank cards. As far as I'm concerned, that's a win."

"Is the journal still in it?" he asked, and she nodded, opening the bag and handing it to him.

"It doesn't look any worse for wear." He ran his hand over the leather cover, then opened the book, scanning the first entry, wanting to know a little more about Ruby. Not through the lens of Ella's love. Through her words, the things she wrote about, what she saw when she looked at the world.

"The book might not, but we all do. I think I've got a pound of ash in my hair, and probably double that in my lungs," Wren commented, striding toward them, her gaze focused on Sam.

She probably wanted an explanation for the hug.

He didn't have one.

Even if he did, he wouldn't have offered it.

He loved his job, but outside of work, he made his own decisions.

"You do know you're still working this case," she said, and he frowned.

She jabbed the book. "You're still on the case, and we like to process evidence in a certain way. Or have you forgotten that we have protocol to follow? Even out here."

Surprised, he met her eyes, saw the humor in her gaze.

She'd reminded him of his purpose there, and she obviously planned to leave it at that.

"I didn't say you could take the book as evidence," Ella said uneasily. "I'm happy to let you read it, but I'm not willing to have it out of my sight."

"Understood," Wren said. "We'll look through it while you're around. If there's anything we want to study further, we'll make copies."

"I appreciate it."

"You know what I'd appreciate?" Radley asked. "Finding the guys who set that fire. And I can guarantee it was more than one person. Look at that place," he gestured toward the burning building, its roof caved in, flames shooting out its windows. "Several fires had to be set at once for that to happen."

"The Organization has plenty of people willing to do their dirty work. Whoever it was, however many people, they had to have a key to get in the front door. I locked it before we went up to Ruby's apartment," Wren said.

"There's a back door," Ella offered, and Wren shook her head.

"It was locked, too. I checked it."

"That means someone with a key walked in with a friend or two and destroyed a million-dollar building, all in the hope of getting rid of a woman who doesn't know anything about how The Organization works? That makes no sense." Radley raked a hand through his hair and a puff of black smoke drifted into the air.

"I'm guessing they're just as anxious to get rid of me," Sam said. "I did infiltrate their syndicate and collect data from their computer systems."

"Or, maybe, our deaths would have just been a nice bonus to what they were really trying to accomplish," Ella said, taking the notebook and slipping it back into her purse.

"You don't think murder was their goal?" Wren asked, her eyes gleaming with interest. She enjoyed bouncing ideas off team members, and she was always willing to keep an open mind.

"I don't know. They could have killed me before they tossed me in the shipping crate. They didn't."

"I think they planned to move you through their trafficking channels. You're young. You're alone. You don't have many people who would be looking for you. Not right away," Sam said, remembering his initial impression of her. She'd looked like a kid, and that was exactly what The Organization trafficked in.

"I don't know how they would have known anything about my life. I've asked a lot of questions, but I haven't answered many."

"But Ruby liked to talk, right? She was a social butterfly, lots of friends?"

"Yes."

"Then it's possible she told people about you. Maybe even shared that you guys were each other's only family."

"I can see that happening," she conceded. "Ruby did love to talk to people, and she had a lot of close friends."

"You were about to explain why you thought the fire might be more than a murder attempt?" Wren prodded, and Ella nodded.

"I wonder if the police department was more interested in Ruby's journals than it pretended to be. Maybe there really was some pejorative information in them. Something that only someone who worked for The Organization would recognize."

"And maybe someone working for the sheriff *and* The Organization saw the information and wanted to get his hands on the journals? So he broke into Ruby's apartment after you were kidnapped and took them?" Sam could see that. He could believe it.

But it still didn't explain the fire.

"Yes. Except I'd put the only important journal in the desk drawer." She tapped her bag. "This is the one that had numbers in some of the margins and three names jotted inside the back cover. None of the other journals had a smudge outside the lines. Ruby was particular about things. A perfectionist. She liked her world neat and orderly. That's why I kept going back to that one journal, and it's why it wasn't with the others. Ruby hid a message in it. Maybe not purposely, but I know it's there. I just need to figure out what she was trying to say."

"We may be able to help you with that," Wren assured her. "Knowing what the message is will help us figure out why the journals are so important."

"Not all the journals. Just one."

"And the guy who grabbed the ones on the shelf realized he didn't have the right one. You and Sam were back in town. The FBI has shown up. And suddenly, The Organization is really desperate to destroy any evidence that might prove their crimes," Wren added. "So, if you can't find the book, burn down the place you think it's hidden."

"I know it sounds far-fetched," Ella began, but Wren raised a hand, stopping the words.

"No. It sounds feasible. Especially if The Organization owns this property, and I suspect it does."

"I asked Adam to check into title records," Sam offered, and she nodded.

"Good. We'll get that information and move on from there, but first, we're going to have to explain things to the local PD." She gestured to a man who was striding toward them, his crisp blue uniform and badge visible beneath his jacket.

"Good morning, folks," he said, his gaze landing and remaining on Sam. "I'm Sheriff Eli Johnson. Damariscotta Police Department. Looks like you were inside the house when the fire started."

"That's right," Sam responded, since the question seemed directed at him.

"You were fortunate to get out," the sheriff noted. "The fire marshal said there were probably ten minutes between the start of the blaze and total consumption of the property."

"It happened fast," Sam agreed, trying to figure out what the guy's game was.

"I guess I should assume you had good reason to be in the building?"

"My cousin has an apartment there," Ella offered. "Or had."

"Right. Ruby McIntire, and you're Ella. We met a few days ago." He offered his hand and a sincere smile, then switched his gaze back to Sam. "You're Sam Rogers?"

"Sheridan."

"That's not the information I have on you."

"I'm surprised you have any information."

"You work for the medical clinic, right?"

"Actually, I'm with the FBI."

"Interesting."

"Why?"

"We got a call about a computer system theft. Someone grabbed a couple of servers from the server room and took off with them. The name Sam Rogers came up when I asked about suspects and motive. Apparently, he worked there for a month and was fired yesterday for being intoxicated on the job."

"You shouldn't believe everything you're told, Sheriff," Sam said. "I did work at the clinic, but I wasn't fired, I didn't steal computer servers and my name isn't really Sam Rogers."

"Like you said, a person shouldn't believe everything he's told. How about you come on down to the station? We'll see if we can get things straightened out there."

"It looks like you have your hands full with the fire," Wren said, pulling her badge out and holding it up for him. "I'm Special Agent Wren Santino. Boston field office. Sam works for me, and I can assure you, he's telling the truth."

"Good." The sheriff's gaze dropped to her badge, then rose to her face. "But I still want to discuss this at my office. There are a lot of people around. I don't know about all of you, but I'd rather them not be privy to this conversation. Do you have a vehicle?"

"We were parked in the driveway," Wren said. She didn't argue with him. She didn't try to bandy her authority around. She liked to play nice with local police.

"Let's get you all checked out by the paramedics, then I'll take two of you in my cruiser. The other two can ride with my deputy. We're parked at the end of the street. The drive won't be long. We're across the Main Street bridge in Damariscotta about six miles outside town."

He strode away, obviously expecting to be followed.

"Thoughts?" Sam asked Wren, and she shrugged.

"Might as well see what's on his mind. I don't think it's those missing servers. You take Ella and ride with him. Radley and I will bum a ride with the deputy."

"And if we don't end up at the sheriff's office?" he asked. He agreed with Wren—this wasn't about missing servers.

"You can handle yourself. I'm sure of that. And if you get driven out into the middle of nowhere again, Honor will be able to find you."

She tossed a smile over her shoulder as she walked away.

Radley followed, and then it was just Sam and Ella standing near the dock. A breeze had picked up, ruffling the hair that had escaped her ponytail. He tucked it behind her ear, letting his fingers linger against her cool skin.

She'd been through enough, and he didn't want to put her through more. If the sheriff was on the up-and-up, a trip to his office was fine. If he wasn't, Sam didn't want Ella anywhere near him.

"I'm thinking I should call Honor and have her give me a lift to the sheriff's office. She can take you back to her place when she's done," he said.

"She's teaching a class, remember?"

"She's working a case. That takes precedence."

"You don't have to worry about me, Sam. I've

been taking care of myself for a long time. I'm pretty good at it."

"Good to know," he said. "But being good at taking care of yourself isn't the same thing as being excellent at staying alive. In situations like this, you're going to want to want to be both. Come on. Let's get moving before the sheriff comes back and cuffs me."

He took her hand. Not because she needed help navigating the flat terrain. Because he wanted to. Because keeping her close to keep her safe had become keeping her close because he enjoyed having her there.

He'd done a lot of things wrong in his life.

He'd planned his course, thinking he had control of it. He'd set a path for his life with Shelly, and when that hadn't panned out, he'd switched direction to follow his career.

But he'd learned a lot working in law enforcement.

He'd learned that time was fleeting, that life was fragile and finite and brief. That opportunities lost couldn't always be regained.

What he'd learned most of all was that God's plan was best, and that faith was the thread that wound shattered hearts together again. People who had it possessed superhuman strength. Not the kind that lifted cars off little kids or stopped a bullet with a bare hand. The kind of deep emotional fortitude that kept them going when others would have given up.

He saw that in Ella. In the way she moved from one crisis to another and didn't crumble. The way she'd navigated the steep slope despite her fear. The way she'd loosened her grip on his hand and trusted that she would fall into safety.

She didn't need him.

He knew that, but he was going to stick around anyway. Until The Organization had been stopped and her cousin's death had been ruled a homicide and she was safe again.

NINE

Ella had been to the sheriff's office several times to discuss Ruby's death, but she'd never been driven there in a squad car. She'd have liked to think of the new experience as an adventure, but she was sitting in the back with Sam, the leather seat reeking of saddle soap and disinfectant. Both odors were faint compared to the strong smell of smoke that clung to her skin and hair.

She wanted to ask the sheriff to open a window, but he was busy navigating through the crowd of onlookers who'd gathered on the street outside the house. The apartment building was iconic. It had been standing in the same spot for over a century.

Now it was gone.

Nothing left but singed support beams and a wet and steaming pile of ashes.

It wasn't surprising that people had questions

or that they were eager for answers. Several tapped the sheriff's window as he rolled past.

He waved but didn't stop.

"If you want to talk to some of these people," Sam said, "we can wait."

"I've got a deputy getting ready to do that. She's better at the public-image thing. Me? I prefer to stay behind the scenes as much as possible." They'd finally reached the end of the crowded road, and he turned left, heading for the bridge that connected Newcastle to the neighboring town. "Hopefully, Victor has good insurance on that place. It can't be replaced, but it would be nice if he could recoup his losses."

"Is Victor the owner?" Sam asked, his hand wrapped around Ella's the way it had been when he was leading her to the squad car.

"His company is."

Sam's grip tightened just enough for Ella to feel his tension. They'd been speculating about The Organization's connection to the apartment building. Maybe he thought he was about to find out the truth.

"What company is that?" His palm pressed against Ella's so firmly she couldn't *not* notice how warm his skin was, how calloused. She wanted to weave her fingers through his and hold on tight.

She'd told him that she didn't need him to keep her safe, and she'd meant it.

But having him around? It was a lot nicer than she'd expected and a lot more addictive.

"You're asking an awful lot of questions for someone who's sitting in the back of a squad car."

"Is there a reason you don't want to answer?"

"Just making a comment." They'd reached the bridge, and he turned onto it. Ella could see tendrils of smoke still drifting up from Ruby's apartment building. If she hadn't fit through the window, if Sam hadn't insisted she do so, if she hadn't seen the chair and pulled it away from the door…

So many things could have gone wrong, but somehow all of them had gone right. She had to trust that would continue. She had to believe that God's plan was being worked out. Despite the trauma and the difficulty.

Despite Ruby's death.

That was the harder one to think about.

A young, faithful, wonderful person had had her life snuffed out, and no matter how much Ella tried, she couldn't think of a purpose for that.

At least, not one that made sense.

God was good all the time. That was one of

Ruby's mantras, but it was hard to see good amid such tragedy.

"You were going to tell me the name of Victor's company," Sam said quietly. Calmly. But she heard a hard edge in his voice.

"I don't recall saying that."

"You didn't. I did. You're a county officer, Sheriff. I'm a federal one. Presumably, we're on the same team. If that's the case, you've got no need to withhold information from me."

"I wasn't planning to. I'm just curious as to why you want to know."

"We're working on a case, and we have an informant who told us this is the place to look if we want to solve it."

"What kind of case?"

"I'll leave it to my supervisor to explain."

"Does it have to do with missing teens and young adults?"

The question made Ella's heart skip a beat. She wanted to shout "yes" at the top of her lungs, but she hadn't been included in the conversation.

"That's right," Sam said.

The sheriff nodded. "That's what I thought. Victor is one of four investors in Medical Properties Incorporated."

"Who are the others?"

"Larry George, Ian Wade and Debra Murphy."

"Ian?" She wasn't sure why she was surprised. Maybe because Ruby had never mentioned that her boyfriend was a major investor in the medical clinic.

"Wade was Ruby's boyfriend, right?" Sam said. "How long had they been dating?"

"Eight or nine months." She remembered Ruby's excited text about the dinner cruise she'd been invited to and the gushing follow-up text saying she'd been asked out again. Ruby didn't do deep relationships, but she'd loved easy romance—dinner and movie dates, hikes through the woods together, bike rides or bowling. Anything that was fun and easy and didn't require too much commitment.

"I think when we're finished this, I'll make a trip to the medical clinic and ask Wade a few questions about his relationship with Ruby," Sam said.

"I'm sure Wade will appreciate that," the sheriff responded, the sarcasm in his voice unmistakable.

"He doesn't have to appreciate it. He just has to cooperate. Do you think he won't?"

"He will as long as it's in his best interest. Otherwise, he'll demand to have an attorney with him. My office has communicated with him several times regarding missing-persons reports that were filed by local businesses who were worried about employees. He was the physician of record in three of the four cases. He was willing to share what he knew, and we were able to gather information without difficulty. But last year we had an anonymous tip that the clinic was dealing in narcotics. Ian wasn't as willing to discuss that."

"He lawyered up?"

"Yes. In the end, we found no evidence that the accusation was true, but it took us four times longer than necessary to determine that."

"Are Wade and the other three investors local to the area?"

"No. I met Ian seven years ago. The town needed a larger medical facility. A local landowner offered a city lot to build on, and the county council accepted bids from a few different companies. Medical Properties had the best plan at the most reasonable price. They broke ground six years ago, and they've been here ever since."

"Are people around here happy about it?" Sam asked.

"That depends on who you ask."

"I'm asking you."

"Most people are happy. We needed the clinic, and it offers sliding-scale services for patients who don't have medical insurance."

"But?"

"In the past two years, we've had fifteen people go missing."

"Citizens of the town?"

"No. Transients. Runaways. Explorers. Adventurers. Whatever name you want to put to them, they're mostly living off the grid and disconnected from whoever they were before they showed up in our town."

"If they're transients, how do you know they disappeared?" Ella asked, taking out Ruby's journal and flipping through it. Her cousin had said something about a kid missing from the rehab group that met on Tuesdays.

"Because they were here one day and gone the next."

"That *is* what transients do," Sam pointed out. "They stop somewhere for a day or for a month. Sometimes longer. And then they leave. As far as I'm aware, they don't provide forwarding addresses or tell everyone goodbye."

"Exactly. We've always had our share of wanderers moving through town. It's a beautiful place, and in the spring, summer and early fall, it's easy to forage for food in the woods or on the river. But in all the time I've been living here—and I've been here every one of my thirty-seven years—I've never known a transient to come to town and leave without his stuff."

"Without his things?" Ella asked, flipping through the pages of the journal.

"Bedrolls. Sleeping bags. Duffel bags. Backpacks. I've had all those things brought to my office and turned into lost and found. I found IDs tucked away in everything that was collected. State IDs or driver's licenses. There was some cash hidden between layers of sleeping bag padding and in the lining of backpacks. Sometimes just a few coins. Old photos of people I couldn't identify. Clothes. Toiletries. Lots of things we'd probably take for granted but that a homeless person would never leave behind. The biggest red flag came from two local business owners who'd reported employees missing when they hadn't shown up for work or collected their last paychecks."

"Would those business owners be willing to speak with me?" Sam asked, and the sheriff nodded.

"I'm sure they would."

"What about the things that were found and turned into your office? Where were they discovered?" Sam asked.

"The public dock. Parks. Playgrounds. The side of the road."

"I'll admit the abandoned paychecks are suspicious, but things are left behind or tossed out car windows all the time," Sam commented.

"Trash might get left behind. The occasional sweater or coat. Banana peels are tossed out windows. Gum is tossed out windows. Fast-food wrappers are tossed out windows. I've even seen shoes tossed out windows, but no one throws a filled backpack out. Not when it contains their ID, their cash, their clothes." The sheriff was adamant, his certainty making the hair on Ella's nape stand on end.

This was what the FBI had been suspecting— The Organization preying on a population no one cared about and that no one would miss.

Only, the sheriff obviously cared, and Ruby had obviously missed at least one person who'd disappeared.

Ella skimmed one page after another. Finally, she found it—close to the end, the note scrawled haphazardly at the bottom of another beautifully written passage.

"Did you keep the items that were turned in?" Sam pulled out his phone and began typing a message to someone.

"No, Sheridan. I took it to the dump, tossed it into the trash pit and washed my hands of it," the sheriff answered sarcastically, his irritation obvious.

"Okay. So you kept it, and I'll assume you used the IDs you found to plug names into the national database of missing persons?"

"I did. And I came up empty. I have fifteen people gone, but apparently not one of them is actually missing."

"Did one of the IDs belong to Eric Bellow?" Ella asked, reading and rereading the name and the three sentences Ruby had written about him.

Eric Bellow. 17 years. Arrived in town September 1. Gone October 30th. Still have the bank info he asked me to keep. Scanned and saved in file.

"How did you know?" the sheriff asked.

"Ruby wrote about him." She touched the name, and Sam leaned close, his focus on the note scribbled at the bottom of the journal entry. Different color of ink. Different style of writing.

"Are you sure she wrote this?" he asked, slipping the notebook from her hands and reading the words aloud. "Because it doesn't look like the rest of her writing."

"She wrote in calligraphy when she was journaling. That—" she touched the page "—is her normal handwriting."

"You're certain?"

"As certain as I can be without hiring a handwriting expert."

"We'll copy this and send it to an expert I know at the Houston field office. Do you have other samples of her writing?"

"I do at my place. She loved snail mail and

sent me handwritten letters every couple of weeks. They're in a box in my closet."

"With your permission, we can send someone into your home to find them."

"Will I get the samples back?"

"Yes," he said, closing the notebook and handing it back to her. "That's an interesting note she left."

"I was going to say the same thing," the sheriff agreed. "Why would he leave his bank account information with Ruby?"

"Because he didn't have a home?" Ella speculated, dropping the journal into her bag. "If he'd gotten a job and received his first paycheck, he'd have had to deposit it in a bank, right? Maybe he opened an account and didn't want to carry the information around with him."

"He'd only need a bank account if he planned to stick around town for a while," the sheriff said. "Otherwise, he could have walked into the Walmart and used their check-cashing service."

"Maybe he did plan to stay in town," Ella said, her mind on the seventeen-year-old. He'd been a kid, really. A child who'd had nowhere to go. No home to return to. Nothing but what he could carry. Maybe he'd wanted to put down roots and stay a while. A job would have been the first step in that direction. A bank account would have been the second.

"That still doesn't explain why he gave bank information to your cousin," the sheriff insisted, turning off the main road that ran through town and onto a side street.

She'd driven it several times, and she knew it wound through a community and then onto a country road that ran parallel to the river.

"Maybe he trusted her," Sam said. "She was his drug-addiction counselor, right?"

"Yes. She mentioned in another entry that he was part of her Tuesday night group last year, but was concerned when he stopped showing up to the meeting."

"It still might be a stretch to think he trusted her enough to hand over his bank account information." The sheriff reached a four-way stop and turned, the river gleaming below. A grassy knoll separated asphalt from tall river grass.

"He was seventeen," Ella reminded him. "He was alone in the world. Maybe he just wanted someone to believe in."

"If so, your cousin was a good person to choose. I don't know if I mentioned this to you when you came to the office, but she and I attended the same church."

"No. You didn't." And if he had, it wouldn't have made any difference to Ella. Her goal was to prove that Ruby hadn't been a drug addict, that her death hadn't been accidental. Nothing anyone said about her cousin, no story anyone told, could have swayed her from that.

"We didn't know each other well, but I never heard a bad word said about her. The kids in her Sunday school class loved her. The ladies in her Bible study group felt the same. As far as I could determine, there's been no gossip about a drug problem or addiction. I talked to a few of Ruby's friends after you came to the office. They were all shocked by her cause of death."

"That doesn't surprise me."

"You knew your cousin. She was merely an acquaintance of mine. When her body was discovered, the situation looked cut-and-dried. Drug paraphernalia. Tourniquet. Needle mark. Unfortunately, my office has processed scenes like that dozens of times. Opioids have been an increasingly virulent problem in the area. In the last few years, the number of drug overdoses has tripled. The number of deaths from drug overdoses has nearly doubled."

"That's a big spike," Sam commented, tapping his fingers impatiently against his thigh.

She almost covered his hand to stop the restless movement, but she couldn't stop remembering how it had felt to throw caution to the wind, to wrap her arms around his waist, let her head rest against his chest, hear the steady pulse of his heart.

She also couldn't stop thinking that she'd be making a big mistake if she fell for Sam.

Big. Huge. Colossal.

Inevitable.

That's what Ruby would have said.

She'd believed in love at first sight, happily-ever-afters, soul mates.

Ella believed in keeping her heart, and her body, intact.

"Like I said, lots of things have changed since Medical Properties Incorporated arrived in town. Not all for the worse. We have a quicker emergency response time for non-critical patients. Better treatment options for low-income citizens. Good doctors and nurses that the community has come to rely on," the sheriff responded, glancing in his rearview mirror and scowling. "You'd think people wouldn't drive a hundred miles an hour on a country road when the sheriff is in front of them."

Sam shifted in his seat and looked out the back window.

Ella did the same.

She could see a car racing toward them. Distant, but closing the gap rapidly. "Wow. He's flying."

"Yeah, and he's going to get a ticket for it if he doesn't slow down," the sheriff muttered.

"Is there a place to turn off around here?" Sam broke in.

"Not really. There are a couple of old dirt roads that lead to hunting cabins, but they narrow quickly and are only accessible by foot or ATV."

"Are they for public use?" Sam asked.

"It's all county land and has been for seventy years."

"So your speeder could be a hunter or camper? Someone who plans to spend some time out in the wilderness."

"Not if he's from around here. There's better hunting farther from town. All the locals know it."

"How far is your office?" Sam was still watching out the back window.

"Four miles." The sheriff accelerated. "Not far."

"It'll be far if the guy behind us has a gun."

"You're armed," the sheriff said.

Sam nodded. "Yes."

"I'm armed. We should be ok—" A car jumped out in front of them, exploding from a hidden road a hundred yards ahead and heading toward them at breakneck speed.

A game of chicken that Ella didn't want to play.

The sheriff swerved, the SUV bouncing off

the road and down the knoll. They were heading straight for the water, and Ella didn't think there was anything he could do about it. They were moving too fast, the brakes locking as he slammed on them.

Sam's hand was on the back of her head, pushing it down between her knees.

He was saying something, but all she could hear was the squeal of brakes and the splash of water as they hit the river.

Momentum carried them out past feathery river grass and gray-green boulders, the SUV finally coming to a stop a dozen yards from shore. Nose down, rear up, cold water already seeping into the front and lapping up against the windows there.

Sam didn't waste time.

He unclipped his seat belt and did the same for Ella, then grabbed the door handle and opened it. The river pulsed just below the doorsill, water splashing up and onto the floorboards.

"You two okay?" Sheriff Johnson asked, releasing his seat belt and opening the glass panel that separated the front of the squad car from the back.

"We'll be better once we're out of here," Sam said, eyeing the water, the shore and the two vehicles idling on the road.

"Agreed. The front end of the SUV is going down fast, and the river is deep enough here to completely submerge it." He tried his radio, shook his head. "Already dead."

"Maybe we should call for help *after* we get out of here?" Ella suggested, her voice shaking.

"It's going to be okay," Sam assured her, wanting to pull her out quickly, help her to shore and get her to safety. But safety didn't exist on shore. Not with the occupants of the cars waiting for them to emerge. They'd set up a nearly perfect ambush, and they were waiting to make certain they took out their targets. With the right person behind the barrel, a high-powered rifle could easily make a shot at this range. Sam knew that. Just like he knew that staying out of the line of fire would be a death sentence. The SUV *would* sink. With or without them in it.

"What do you think?" Sheriff Johnson asked. "Do we risk it?"

"We don't have much of a choice."

"We could wait for total submersion, and then exit underwater. That will make their target practice more difficult."

"Good plan unless our timing is off. Then one or more of us could drown." The truth was, if Ella weren't with him, Sam would have taken the risk. He was a strong swimmer, and he wasn't prone to panic. But she *was* with him, and she looked terrified, eyes wide in her soot-streaked face.

"First fire and now water. If we'd had them both at the same time, the apartment building would still be standing," she murmured, her eyes focused on the cars that were still waiting. "They don't seem very eager to leave, but I sure am."

She pulled her purse strap over her head and scrambled for the door, the large bag slapping against her chest as she lunged in its direction.

Sam grabbed her by the waist, tugging her back.

"Wait until we have a plan," he growled, holding her still when she tried to escape his grip.

"If you want me to wait, you'd better come up with one fast, because my plan is not to drown in a police car in a river that has a name I can barely spell!"

"You're panicking," he said calmly. "And that's not going to help."

"No. I'm taking action, because every minute we sit in this vehicle increases our chances of not getting out of it. The water is freezing, Sheriff Johnson is chest deep in it and we all know muscles cease functioning when the body gets too cold. Blood is pumped out of the extremities and into the major organs, but eventually even that isn't enough. The—"

"You sound like you've been watching a lot of documentaries," the sheriff commented, pulling his keys from the ignition and using a small tool dangling from the chain to break the front passenger window.

"I wrote an article on the long-term effects of hypothermia a couple of years back. Since this might be my last opportunity to spout useless trivia, I decided I'd better take it."

Sam laughed.

He couldn't help himself.

Even terrified, she had a sense of humor and a wry way of viewing the world that made him smile.

"Not so useless," the sheriff said. "Because you're right. Sitting in cold water isn't going to do anything but weaken us. I'll go out the passenger side of the vehicle and see if I can distract them. You two wait a few seconds and exit through the open door." He slipped through the broken window, splashing loudly as he swam away from the SUV.

The occupants of the cars didn't notice or didn't care.

Not surprising.

Sam and Ella were their targets.

The front end of the vehicle dropped lower,

water pouring in through the window and splashing over the seat. It lapped over the doorjamb and swished around Sam's feet.

"I really think we need to go," Ella said uneasily.

"Are you a strong swimmer?"

"Strong enough to get myself to shore," she assured him, already slipping into the water.

He followed, the river icy and sharp, the fall air warm in comparison. On the side of the road, he could see the cars' doors still closed, sunlight glinting on the windows. He couldn't see the occupants, but he assumed there was more than one in each vehicle.

Ella was treading water. White skin. Purple lips. Gasping breaths.

"Which way?" she asked.

The far bank was at least a quarter mile away. On a warm summer day that would be an easy swim, but today it could kill them.

"Straight into the shore. Aim for that area." He gestured toward a small peninsula of land, lush with river grass thick and tall enough to provide cover.

She nodded, her chin dipping beneath the water as she started paddling, the sound of screaming sirens suddenly filling the air.

TEN

The peninsula wasn't that far, and Ella should have been able to make it there easily. As a kid, she'd spent hours swimming in the pond behind her grandmother's house. As a high school student, she'd spent most of her summers working as a lifeguard at a local pool.

She'd always been an excellent swimmer.

Until now.

She kicked frantically, trying to gain some momentum, but her movements were sluggish and uncoordinated, her muscles too cold to react properly. *This* was what she'd been babbling about in the sinking SUV—the insidiousness of the cold, the way it seeped into the body and shut it down.

She'd been babbling about it, but she hadn't realized she was about to experience it. She slipped under, water rushing into her nose and mouth, her purse strap wrapped around her neck and nearly choking her, but she tried her best to hold it above the water.

Sam dragged her out of the water, one arm wrapped around her waist, fingers digging into her abdomen. Water dripped into her eyes and off her chin, her hair pasted to her cheeks and neck.

He set her down, her feet sinking into mud, long grass brushing her shins. She was out of the water, on her feet, staring at Sam's soaked black T-shirt, and she wasn't sure how she'd gotten there.

"Okay?" he asked, brushing hair from her cheeks, tilting her chin so he could look in her eyes. She was staring into his face, and she couldn't make herself look away, couldn't make herself *move* away.

"Yes. Thanks." Her throat still burned from the fire, her voice was hoarse and she was shivering, but all she could think about, all she could focus on, was him.

That couldn't be good.

It *wasn't* good.

She didn't want to open her heart again.

She didn't want to be hurt again.

She didn't want to believe in all the old dreams again or let herself imagine how wonderful it would be to love someone who loved her back. Not faked or pretended or feigned it.

She made herself step away, forced her gaze from Sam to the road. The cars were gone, replaced by a police cruiser. Lights flashing, doors open. Several people were running across the grassy knoll, sprinting down the hill and straight toward them. She recognized Wren and Radley. A third man was with them—tall and lean, his dark suit and white dress shirt incongruent against the backdrop of river grass and water. She guessed him to be another agent, his movements just as fluid and controlled as his coworkers'. A uniformed officer ran behind him, black boots spraying water and mud, face shadowed by a uniform hat.

"Where's Sheriff Johnson?" he called, and Ella realized what she hadn't before. She and Sam were alone on the peninsula, the river empty, the SUV already sucked beneath is surface.

She scanned the shore and then the lake again, but she saw no sign of the sheriff.

"He's out," Sam responded.

He didn't sound concerned, but Ella was.

The moment she'd dropped into the water, she'd known she was in trouble, the quick sharp sting of cold stealing her breath and her thoughts. She'd barely been able to swim.

She *hadn't* been able to swim.

If Sam hadn't dragged her to shore, she'd

probably be lying on the sediment-covered bottom of the river. Since the sheriff had exited the vehicle first, he should have exited the water first. If he hadn't, something was wrong.

Had he succumbed to the cold?

Drowned, when his neurons short-fired and his muscles refused to cooperate?

Cold wind rippled across the glassy surface of the water, and she held her breath, praying that the sheriff would appear, somewhere close to land.

Even better, on land.

Dripping wet, but safe.

That he'd usher them all to his office and ask questions about the fire, Ruby, The Organization.

"Out of the SUV? Or out of the river?" the officer demanded.

"Both. He exited the water over there." Sam pointed toward two pine trees that jutted out over the river, their needles carpeting the ground. "I saw him running toward the road and then lost sight of him. Based on where he was heading, I'd say he was trying to get a better look at the cars that ambushed us."

"Ambushed?" Wren had reached them, her face still streaked with soot, her expression grim.

"Yeah." Sam explained quickly, the quiet cadence of his voice drifting over Ella.

She was tired.

Bone-deep exhausted.

And she wanted to go home to the predicable world of research, deadlines and edits.

"How are you holding up?" Radley asked, appearing at her side with a blanket in one hand and a cell phone in the other.

"Fine," she lied, and he nodded.

"So not good?" He dropped the blanket around her shoulders and glanced at his phone. "Our ride will be here in three minutes. We'll get you somewhere safe so you can warm up."

"What ride?"

"Honor," Wren answered. "She and Radley are going to escort you to a safe house where you'll remain until the threat against you is neutralized."

"What about Sam?" The question popped out, and she knew what it told everyone standing there about how she felt.

Wren eyed her thoughtfully, her gaze intent and her expression neutral. Whatever she thought or felt, she hid it well. "He'll join you when we finish here."

"I appreciate the offer of a safe house, but I'd rather go home. I've already been here nearly a week, and I have deadlines to meet." She did. She also had her quiet house, her sanctuary with window alarms and three locks on every exte-

rior door. Once she was there, she'd be able to
think more clearly about Ruby, her journals,
her death.

And about Sam.

He was talking to the officer, the two of them
striding along the shoreline, heading toward the
area where the sheriff had last been seen. He
glanced back, his blond hair dark with moisture, his jaw stubbled with the beginnings of a
beard. Hard face, hard expression and too much
muscle. If she'd seen him in a dark alley, she'd
have run in the opposite direction.

She'd have probably done the same if she'd
spotted him in a well-lit one.

Now, she wanted to run toward him and stay
close.

That was completely out of character, completely not her normal MO. She liked physical
space. She liked solitude. She enjoyed sitting by
herself and listening to her thoughts. But Sam
intrigued her. The way he worked with confidence and compassion. The ease with which
he moved from one crisis to another, without
panic or confusion or fear. He was the kind of
person who'd be great on any team—a leader
who wouldn't insist on leading but wouldn't re-
fuse the role, one who did rather than delegated.

She liked that.

She liked him.

And that could lead to trouble if she let it.

She looked away, focusing her attention on Wren.

The special agent was watching her, dark eyes focused and intense, expression unreadable. She didn't seem like the kind of person to miss many details, and Ella suspected she was excellent at reading body language and facial expressions.

She tried to school hers into one of abject indifference. "You have my information. If you need to contact me once I'm home, there won't be a problem."

She lifted her purse, pulling the strap back over her head, doing everything she could to act like she wasn't falling hard for one of Wren's agents.

"It isn't in your best interest to return to Charlotte."

"Or in the best interest of your case?" She opened the purse, relieved to see that the interior wasn't filled with water. Her cell phone was functional, the screen glowing. She took out the journal. The cover was water stained but the inside had mostly been spared. Only the edges of the paper were wet. "I'm still going to cooperate, Agent Santino. I just want to do it from a more comfortable location."

"I think you'll find the safe house very comfortable. The place is a summer rental with three master suites. Fireplaces. A large kitchen."

"That's not what I mean by comfortable." And she was certain Wren knew that.

"I know," Wren conceded. "But it's currently all we have to offer."

"You could offer me a ride to Charlotte. Or to the nearest airport."

"I could, but I wouldn't feel good about it. You may think you'll be safer in Charlotte, but you won't be. The Organization is far-reaching, and it has plenty of people on the payroll. I'd hate for something to happen to you because you didn't take the threat seriously."

"I'm taking it seriously."

"Then stay in the safe house for the next few days. Let us do the jobs we've been trained to do."

It was a reasonable request, and Ella knew she'd be foolish to deny it. She wanted to be alone. She wanted time to think. She wanted her house and her bed and her scuffed writing desk.

She also wanted to live.

She wanted to find out the truth about what had happened to Ruby. Whether they were behind Ruby's death or not, she wanted The Organization stopped.

"Okay," she agreed. "I'll stay there for a couple days."

"Is there anything you'd like us to bring you from home? If so, I can have a Charlotte police officer retrieve it, and we can have it for you by tomorrow."

"The only thing I'd like to have is my laptop, and I left that under the seat of the station wagon."

"As far as I know, they haven't found your vehicle yet, but when they do, I'll get the laptop. In the meantime, we can set you up with another one. Adam?" she called, and the man in the dark suit walked over.

"Ella, this is Special Agent Adam Whitfield. He's with the Special Crimes Unit," Wren said.

"Adam." He smiled and offered a firm handshake. "I was sorry to hear that you recently lost your cousin. I know how painful it is to have to say goodbye to someone you love."

"Thank you," she replied.

"She needs a laptop," Wren cut in. "Can you arrange that?"

"Of course."

"And we need an update on her car from the local PD. Her personal laptop is in it."

"So is Ruby's," Ella added. "I had a box of her stuff behind the back seat. Her laptop and weekly planner were in it."

Wren raised a brow, her expression as neutral

and unreadable as ever. "Did you find anything interesting in either?"

"She'd jotted a few notes in the planner. I thought they might be birth dates for people in her recovery groups. They were always penned in on Tuesday or Thursday, and that's when the groups met."

"She wrote birth dates? Or the names of people who had birthdays?" Wren asked.

"Birth dates. Or…just dates. I really don't know what they represented. She had a day and year written in on the Tuesday before she died. I remember that specifically because it was so close to her death, and I kept going back to it, wondering if it was connected somehow."

"I'll look into it," Wren promised, jotting something into a small notebook she pulled from her pocket. "How about the laptop? Did you find anything on it that you thought important?"

"I couldn't unlock it. I don't know her password. I was hoping I'd find it somewhere in the apartment, but if it was there, it's gone now."

"Honor can probably unlock the system," Adam said. "She's an expert at computer technology. Let me see if I can get the local PD a little more excited about finding your car. I want to take a look at the dates." He strode away, and Ella ran her hand over the notebook again, wiping away a few drops of water that had fallen from her hair. "The sheriff mentioned that there's been a problem with people going missing from the area."

"That coincides with the information we have about The Organization's activities."

"One of them is someone Ruby mentioned in her journal. I'm not sure how important that is, but it's probably best if you take this into protective custody."

She handed it to Wren. "Being around me seems to be hazardous."

"It won't be once you're in the safe house, but I would like to send this to our evidence lab. They may see something you haven't in Ruby's writing. We'll return it as soon as they finish their analysis." She glanced at the street, gesturing toward a dark SUV that was pulling up next to the squad car. "It looks like your ride is here. We'll talk more at the safe house. For now, get warmed up and get some rest. The past few weeks have been hard ones." She headed back up the hill, and Ella followed, cold despite the blanket.

Getting warm sounded great, but she'd rather stick around and get answers.

The FBI had other ideas.

Honor was out of the SUV before Ella reached it.

She opened the back door. No smile. No

cheerful greeting. Her normal bubbly personality replaced by a more somber persona. "I've got an extra blanket in the back. Climb in. I'll grab it for you."

"I'm fine," Ella said, but Honor hurried to the back and opened the hatch, unzipping a black duffel that sat there. "This is my emergency preparedness kit. Basically two changes of clothes. Blanket." She took it out and tossed it to Ella. "Backup phone. Extra battery. First-aid kit... Here it is! Chocolate." She tossed that, too, the chocolate bar sailing over the seat and into Ella's lap.

"I can't eat your emergency chocolate."

"I can't have you passing out if we have an emergency and have to ditch the ride." She zipped the duffel, closed the hatch and slid in behind the wheel. "You didn't eat this morning, right?"

"Right, but—"

"Eat the chocolate. Not because I'm expecting to be in a footrace with Organization thugs, but because if I am, I want to be sure I don't have to carry you on my back." She started the engine, flipping the heat on to full power as Radley climbed in next to Ella.

"We're set," he said. "Let's head out."

"What about the sheriff?" Ella asked, trying to see details of the scene below. Wren was standing in the tall grass, talking to a uniformed officer. A few feet away, Sam and Adam were pointing at tire marks dug deep into the wet earth.

"He followed the ambush vehicles and was able to get a partial plate on one of them. He's heading to his office to run it with the model and make, and see if he can get a match."

"I'm glad he's okay."

"I'm sure he is, too," Honor said. "We're fortunate that the sheriff's vehicle was the only real casualty. Things could have ended a lot more tragically."

Like they had for Ruby?

Ella hadn't allowed herself to dwell on that. She'd focused her energy on trying to prove that Ruby hadn't been an addict and hadn't died of an accidental overdose. That had been easy before Sam outlined the FBI's theory about her death.

Now, she couldn't stop thinking about it.

Maybe because the car had gone silent. Maybe because all the chaos and the fear was over, and she was left with nothing but her own thoughts. And they were all for Ruby—the loving person she'd been and the tragedy of her loss.

Her cell phone buzzed, and she pulled it

from her purse, glad for the distraction. A text had come through, the number unfamiliar, the words:

Ella? It's Sam. Add me to your address book. If you need anything, let me know.

I need to know if she suffered, she responded, hitting Send before she could rethink the text.

She was unconscious before she knew anything was wrong, was his immediate response.

And then, as if he knew she was noticing the fact that he hadn't answered yes or no to her question:

How she lived was more important than how she died. Remember that. Also remember that I'm going to find the guy who killed her, and I'm going to make sure he pays for it. That won't bring Ruby back, but I think she'd be happy to know that justice was served.

He was right. On both counts. Ruby's life had been everything she'd wanted—fun and adventurous and filled with service to others. Her death had been violent and too soon, but Ruby would have been happy to know that there were people fighting for the truth and that, one day, justice would be served.

"Is everything okay?" Radley asked.

"Yes," she responded by rote.

"Then why do you look like it's not?"

"It's been an exhausting couple of weeks."

"That's the understatement of the century." He unfolded Honor's blanket and draped it across her legs. "But you're not alone in this anymore, Ella. You've got a lot of people standing with you."

"Wow, Radley," Honor said. "That's the nicest thing I've ever heard you say."

"Then you haven't heard me say much, because I have it on good authority that I'm a nice guy."

"Being nice and saying nice things aren't the same," she argued. They sounded like bickering siblings, and that reminded Ella of her early teenage years, the days when Ruby had been in college and they'd squabbled good-naturedly about clothes and hair scrunchies. Their grandmother had still been alive then, and she'd reminded them often that they needed to be nice to each other, because faith and family were the only things that could really be counted on.

She'd been right.

The older Ella got, the more she understood that.

And now, with Ruby gone, she felt the truth of it even more. Ruby had been the only one left in the world who knew her favorite color, the only one who knew she preferred vanilla to chocolate and pie to cake.

The only one who would have noticed if Ella had disappeared.

Ella had never minded that she didn't have a large group of friends or an impressive network of acquaintances. She hadn't ever felt that she needed anyone in her corner. Maybe because Ruby had always been there.

Now, though, her aloneness was like a dripping faucet in the middle of a quiet night. She couldn't ignore it, couldn't turn it off, couldn't tell herself that it didn't matter.

If Sam and the Special Crimes Unit hadn't stepped in, she'd be gone—trafficked out of the country and sold to the highest bidder—or dead.

Radley was right. She wasn't alone. She had people standing with her.

Her phone buzzed again.

You okay? Sam asked.

Probably going to be, she replied.

You WILL be.

Okay, she typed, I concede that I will.

Will you also concede that having dinner together after this is over is a good idea?

Dinner?

Yes. The meal after lunch and before bed, he replied.

And she could picture him typing rapidly, a half smile curving his lips and softening his features.

A couple of weeks ago, she'd have rebuffed the offer, but Ruby's death had changed her.

Or, maybe, meeting Sam had.

Until she'd spent time with him, she hadn't realized how exhausting spending time with Jarrod had been. Sure, after he'd attacked her, she'd known he was an abuser. She'd known he'd put on a pretty facade and that she'd fallen for it. But she hadn't realized that she'd been putting on an act, too. She hadn't realized how hard she'd had to work to feel happy around him, or how easily she'd allowed herself to see the world through his distorted view.

And dinner after this was over? It wasn't a lifetime commitment or a vow of undying loyalty. It was simply two people sitting at a table getting to know one another.

Where would we go? she typed before she could talk herself out of it.

Anywhere that makes you smile.

That would be just about any place where I'm not being kidnapped, shot at or burned alive.

Then probably not anywhere in Newcastle. Which limits my choices to any other place on earth. It'll take time, but I'll figure something out. See you in a few hours.

His response made her smile, and she knew he'd intended it to. Sam looked tough and intimidating, but he had a good heart. One that she couldn't help being attracted to.

Ruby would have loved that.

She'd have loved knowing that Ella had finally found someone who chased the bad memories so far down into her mind that new ones could be formed. She'd have loved hearing every detail of the relationship, and she would have asked a million questions that she'd have demanded Ella answer. She would have played mother and father and concerned elder sister, and then she'd have given the relationship her stamp of approval, because she would have met Sam and loved him.

Ella blinked back tears, dropping the phone into her bag and leaning her head against the seat. She missed Ruby more than she could express.

But, if she let herself, she could feel her presence, see her broad grin and bright eyes, and she could remember that they weren't separated forever. They'd just said goodbye for a little while.

ELEVEN

A week after she'd arrived at the safe house, Ella was six-days past ready to leave.

She was bored, restless and ready to go home, but Sam and his coworkers weren't ready to let her. They'd spent the past week working diligently to find answers to Ruby's death and to Ella's kidnapping. They had a few leads and a little evidence, but not enough of either. Until they found more, Ella was stuck in a huge rental cabin in the middle of the Maine wilderness. If she'd been able to walk outside, it wouldn't have been that bad, but she was confined to the four walls of the structure.

Just to be safe. Sam had said that dozens of times. The words had been repeated even more by Wren, Honor and Radley. She understood their concern, but she was ready to go home, get back to her routine and move on with her life.

She glanced at the clock on the bedside table. One a.m., and she was awake again.

She walked to the window, opening the curtains and looking out into the darkness. Exterior lights illuminated the manicured yard. Beyond that patch of cut grass, trees stood side by side—silent sentries standing guard against an unseen threat.

She let the curtains fall back into place and tried to still her mind, empty her thoughts and free herself from worries so that she could sleep.

She hated this time of morning more than any other. Every creak of floorboards, every soft tap of the wind against the window, every sound made her heart jump. She'd broken up with Jarrod on a night like this. A night when everything seemed safe and normal. A night when she could hear the wind whistling beneath the eaves of her house and the muted sound of traffic through the windows.

She shuddered, checking the lock on the windows and then walking out into the hall. She knew she didn't have to check the door locks. She knew that Sam's team had handled it. Just like they had every night since she'd arrived.

She knew it, but she wanted to check anyway. Just in case.

She walked through a wide hallway, careful to avoid a few floorboards that she knew creaked. She didn't want to wake anyone. She sure didn't want to explain why she planned to check the locks in a safe house.

Obviously, the place was secure.

She'd been told the rules when she'd arrived—stay away from windows, keep the curtains drawn, never ever walk outside alone.

But there were no rules about walking around the house in the early hours of the morning or checking the door locks, because she couldn't feel safe if she didn't.

The front door was at the bottom of a curved staircase. She walked to it, checking the lock three times before she was ready to go to the back door.

She headed that way, moving quietly through the dark hallway that led to the back of the house. She reached the kitchen and was happy to see that the light above the stove was glowing, the curtains pulled across the window above the sink, the room quiet and empty. She hurried across the room.

"Going somewhere?" Sam asked, his voice sudden and unexpected.

She whirled around, her heart hammering in her chest.

From surprise and from pleasure, because

her pulse always seemed to race when she was near him.

"You're up late," she said, a little too breathlessly.

"It's my night to pull security shift. How about you?"

"Just checking the locks."

"You do that every night," he commented, opening one of the cupboards and pulling out coffee grounds.

"It's habit."

"Because of what happened with your ex?" He said it casually, as if they'd spoken about it dozens of times before.

"I shouldn't have mentioned him to you," she murmured, her face hot.

"Are you embarrassed that you did?" he asked, and she shook her head.

"Why would I be?"

"Because your face is red." He touched her cheek, his palm cool and callused.

"Jarrod isn't my favorite subject to discuss," she confessed, stepping back so that his hand fell away.

Because she could have stood there forever, staring into his eyes, feeling his cool palm against her heated skin, and she didn't want to be that weak again. Not the way she had been with Jarrod, where she'd given up so much of who she was to be what she'd thought he needed.

"Good, because I'm not that fond of discussing him, either," he responded, and she smiled.

Just like she always seemed to when she was around Sam.

"Do you always say the right thing, Sam?"

"Not always. Probably not even often, but with you, I'd like to try."

"There you go again," she muttered, flicking on the coffee machine because, otherwise, she'd continue staring into his eyes.

"You don't have to be afraid, Ella," he said, handing her the coffee grounds and leaning against the counter as she started the pot.

"I'm not."

"But you check the doors every night, and you avoid my eyes every time you think I'm getting too close."

"I'm cautious. And there's nothing wrong with that."

"No, there isn't. I'd just hate for you to miss out on life because you're too afraid to live it."

"You sound like Ruby," she said, turning to face him again.

"Thank you," he responded, and she couldn't help looking into his eyes. Really looking. He wasn't anything she'd ever dreamed of, and he was nothing like what she should want. He wasn't safe, predicable or easy, and yet, she'd still said she would go to dinner with him once all this was over.

"Sam—"

"What? You don't think this is going to work? You think we're getting in too deep? You want to go back to your life and forget we met?"

"I don't want to forget we met. I'm just not sure this is the right time to be thinking about things like...dinner."

"Everyone has to eat," he said with an easy smile.

"That's the truth."

"And so is this—I'm not going let you be hurt again, Ella. Not by The Organization. Not by your ex. And certainly not by me."

He meant it. She knew he did.

And when he took her hand and tugged her closer, she didn't resist. She didn't pull back as he moved close. She didn't back up as he leaned in.

She didn't do anything but stand where she was, frozen in place, caught in the power of his words and in his gaze.

"Sam," she began, desperate to break the connection that seemed to be forming between them. Terrified of what it might mean and where it might lead.

"Everything is going to be okay," he said,

touching her cheek so gently, her eyes filled with tears.

"You've said that before," she reminded him.

"And I've been right before," he replied, leaning down so that they were just a breath away.

She could see the blond tips of his lashes and the flecks of silver in his eyes. She could see him, and the truth of who he was. Right there in the depth of his gaze. He wasn't like Jarrod. He wasn't like anyone she'd ever known. He was Sam. Strong. Determined. Caring. If she was looking for a relationship, if she wanted to risk her heart again, he'd be the person she'd risk it with.

When his lips brushed her forehead, she didn't move away. Even though she knew she should, even though she didn't really believe that everything would be okay between them. Love hurt. A lot.

She'd learned that, and she'd learned from it. She didn't want to repeat her mistakes. Not even with Sam.

But, when his hands cupped her nape, when his fingers wove through her hair, she didn't stop him.

She leaned closer, her hands resting tentatively on his waist, her fingers curved against soft fabric and firm muscle.

And when he kissed her?

She felt it deep in the place in her heart that had been walled up and closed off since Jarrod.

His phone rang, the insistent sound dragging Sam from the softness of Ella's lips, from the silkiness of her hair, from a mistake he wouldn't regret. One he'd make a thousand more times, if he were given the opportunity.

He pulled back, breathless, spellbound. By her and by this moment. By all the things he felt when he looked into her eyes.

"Wow," she whispered, and he smiled, brushed a strand of hair from her cheek.

"Agreed."

"I didn't mean the kiss," she murmured, her cheeks pink.

"Neither did I," he responded truthfully, his phone going silent and then ringing again.

"Maybe you should get that?" she asked, her hands trembling as she took mugs from a cupboard and filled them with steaming coffee.

She was right. He should.

But he'd have just as soon ignored it.

There was more he wanted to say to her.

A lot more. About how impressed he was by her persistence and bravery, about how much he admired her determination to get justice for Ruby. About how beautiful he found her smile and her intelligence and her laughter.

He pulled his phone from his pocket anyway, glancing at the number.

"It's Adam," he said, and she nodded, handing him a cup of coffee and taking a sip from the one she'd poured herself.

He answered quickly, his gaze still on Ella as she took a seat at the table, her silky hair brushing against her cheek as she leaned across the table and grabbed a packet of sugar from a bowl.

"Hello?" He sounded gruffer than he'd intended, his voice raspy and a little rough.

"You sound happy to hear from me," Adam responded. He'd been staying in Honor's apartment, working with the local PD, conducting interviews with people who'd known Ruby and who worked at the clinic. Wren and Radley joined him during the day. Thus far, they'd hadn't come up with any new evidence, but Honor had managed to trace the emails Sam had received to a computer used by doctors at the clinic. There was no way of knowing who had set up the account or sent the missives, but the information had brought the team a step closer to pinpointing a suspect. They'd obtained a warrant and confiscated several computer hard drives. Computer forensic experts were searching them for evidence that might help bring The Organization down.

"It's one thirty in the morning," Sam said. "Most people are asleep."

"That's fortunate for them, right? We're working, though."

"We? As far as I knew, you were tucked into bed at Honor's place."

"I was. Until Bo Williams called."

Sam's pulse leaped, and he glanced at Ella. "He contacted you?"

"He's been staying at an apartment in Damariscotta, but this evening his wife thought she saw someone from The Organization outside the complex. She's terrified, and he's ready to turn himself in."

"For what? We were already aware of the money laundering, and we gave him immunity for his cooperation."

"He moved Ella's car."

"When?"

"The night she was kidnapped. And—you're going to love this—Ian Wade asked him to do it. He walked into Bo's pawnshop with a fist full of cash and instructions for getting rid of the car. Bo hot-wired it and did what he'd been asked. He didn't think much about it until the police started canvassing the area, looking for it. That's when he decided to leave town."

"He didn't go very far."

"Where else would he go? He's been in the

area for fifteen years. His wife was born here. It's what they know. Besides, he was sure we were searching for him. He figured the immunity thing was off the table since he was complicit in the kidnapping after the fact. He said he'll bring me to the car after we outline a plan to keep his wife and kids safe. He said he's sent them to stay with his in-laws in Portland, but he wants a safer location."

"Did you tell Wren?"

"You're security shift tonight, so I thought I'd let you know. You can fill everyone else in. I'm heading over to Bo's apartment now."

"Are you bringing him here?"

"That depends on what Wren says. Have her give me a call once she's up to speed."

"All right." He was already jogging up the steps, heading for Wren's room. She must have heard him. Her door flew open before he knocked, and even at one in the morning, even fresh out of bed, she looked ramrod straight and ready for action. Black yoga pants. Tight-fitting black shirt. No shoes, and her hair was down. But her eyes were bright, her gaze sharp.

"What's going on?" she asked.

He filled her in quickly, knocking on Radley and Honor's doors as he did so. Minutes later, they were sitting in the kitchen, cups of coffee in front of them, discussing the possible ramifications of bringing Bo to the safe house.

"I don't like it," Wren said, tapping her fingers on the tabletop. "It seems awfully convenient that Bo is suddenly eager to help us find that car. We've been looking for a week."

"So you're not buying the story that his wife saw someone from The Organization?" Honor asked, taking a sip of her coffee and grimacing. "Man, this is strong!"

"Do you want some cream?" Ella asked. She'd been standing a few feet away, hip against the counter, silently listening. There'd been no reason to ask her to leave. She was as involved in this as anyone, and her safety was their utmost concern.

"Nah. A few packets of sugar should do it." Honor grabbed four, ripped them open and dumped them into her cup. "There. Much better. So, do you buy the story, Wren?"

"No. But I'd like to know why he's telling it."

"A threat, maybe?" Radley suggested. "If I had a family, that would be the one way to get to me. Threaten my wife or my kids."

"So let's assume Wade threatened Bo's family. What is he trying to get from him?" Wren asked.

"Me or Ella," Sam answered.

"For what purpose?" Radley asked. "We're

already investigating the clinic, and seeing as how we served a warrant and confiscated several computer systems, I'm pretty certain he knows it."

"Revenge?" Ella said quietly. "The medical clinic has been here for six years. It's probably been a cover for The Organization since then. I arrived in town, started asking questions and ruined what was probably a very lucrative business."

"And we sure didn't help it grow," Wren said. "Whatever the purpose for this meeting, I want it to happen. I'm going to call Adam and tell him to transport Bo here."

"That's not a good idea," Sam said, the thought of Bo being anywhere near Ella filling him with dread.

He knew the guy.

He'd spoken to him on several occasions, and he'd found him to be sleazy and underhanded. Sure, he'd turned informant, but that was only because he hadn't wanted to get caught up in a kidnapping scheme that could put him in jail for life. He might have some moral compunction about preying on kids, but Sam thought his main motivation for going to the FBI was self-preservation.

"I disagree." Wren stood and brushed a few pieces of lint from her yoga pants. "Bo may be the key to arresting Ian Wade. We're close to having enough evidence from the computers, but we need more, and if Wade happened to show up here and make a bid for revenge—"

"We have a civilian here," he reminded her sharply, and she glanced at Ella and nodded.

"We also have five federal officers who are more than capable of protecting her."

"Look, Wren, I'm not one to argue with your plans—"

She smiled. "Yes, you are. If you don't think they're reasonable. I appreciate that about you, but we have close to twenty missing teens in Boston. Fifteen missing from Newcastle and the surrounding area. How many more kids are going to go missing before we stop these guys? If bringing Bo here gives us a chance to bring in one of the kingpins of The Organization, it's a risk we can't afford not to take."

She was right.

He didn't like it, but he couldn't deny it.

"I think Honor should take Ella to her place until this is over," he said.

"She'll be in as much danger there," Honor replied. "There isn't anyone in town who doesn't know you and I are with the FBI, and The Organization would be stupid not to have someone watching my apartment."

"Then take her to Boston."

"That's a waste of time and energy," Ella cut in. "If I survived being kidnapped, shot at, nearly burned alive and almost drowned, I can survive a few hours with a guy like Bo."

"It's not Bo I'm worried about."

"Ian isn't going to get anywhere near me. Not with you around. Besides, God is the one who decides things, and I think this was decided weeks ago. The Organization is going to go down, and I'm not going to stand in the way of that happening."

"Ella, I don't think you understand how much danger—"

"I do understand. But there are some things that have to be done. No matter how much danger is involved. You do what you have to do to shut down The Organization. I'll be in my room. Staying away from the windows. Let me know when it's over."

She walked away.

He almost followed. She'd been hurt before. He didn't want her to ever be hurt again.

But she was right.

Some things had to be done. No matter the risk or the cost. He'd make certain she stayed in her room, that she stayed safe, because he couldn't imagine any other outcome. He couldn't imagine life without her in it.

That was something he needed to think about.

But right now, there were other things that needed his attention.

Wren was on the phone talking to Adam. Honor and Radley were sketching out a plan to beef up security, and Sam was ready to do what Ella had suggested—whatever he had to do to shut down The Organization.

No more missing kids.

No more innocent victims.

No more secrets and lies hidden behind the facade of a medical clinic.

That's what he needed to focus on, what he needed to work for.

He took a seat next to Honor, listening as she listed the safe house's weaknesses, the areas of biggest concern, the places most likely to be breached. They were planning for an attacking army, but he was hoping it would be an army of one.

Ian Wade was one of four investors in Medical Properties Incorporated. He knew the inner workings of the company, and he knew just how deeply it was connected to The Organization. With him in custody, they might be able to get the information that would allow them to cut The Organization off at the knees, cripple it for good and keep it from preying on the vulnerable, the lonely and the forgotten.

That and keeping Ella alive were the goals.

Now they just had to come up with a plan that would ensure both outcomes.

TWELVE

At first, it was quiet. Not even the hushed sound of voices drifting from below. No feet on hardwood floors. No doors opening and closing. Ella sat in the center of her room, away from the windows and the door. Tense. Scared. Wondering if she'd made the wrong decision.

She could be on her way to Boston, instead of sitting in a fancy log cabin in the middle of nowhere, waiting for trouble to come.

But she hadn't wanted Sam and his team to be shorthanded. She'd been worried that Bo would arrive and bring an entire army with him, that somehow the person who was escorting Ella to Boston would be the only one who could save the day.

A silly thought, and she knew it.

But it had been there with the other—that she hadn't wanted to leave Sam. She hadn't wanted to say goodbye, not knowing if she would see him again.

She glanced at the clock.

It had been fifty minutes since Adam called.

Forty minutes since she'd walked into her room and shut the door. Twenty minutes since she'd decided sitting on the floor would make her less of a target than sitting on the bed would.

As if anyone could see through the thick curtains or the walls.

She pulled her knees up to her chest, resting her forehead on the soft flannel pajama bottoms Honor had brought her. Bright orange with smiling yellow faces, they were exactly the kind of thing Ruby would have chosen.

Her cousin would have fit in well with the Special Crimes Unit. She'd have called the chaos an adventure and the danger exciting. She'd have weathered it all with a smile on her face, because that was how Ruby did everything.

She hadn't just lived life. She'd enjoyed every minute, every relationship, every job. She was the person Ella had always wanted to be when she grew up—strong, confident and compassionate.

And now, she was gone.

"I miss you, Ruby," she whispered, wishing she had the journal she'd given to Wren. It was the one thing that hadn't been destroyed in the fire, the one piece of her cousin that hadn't disappeared.

"Ella?" Sam knocked and opened the door, stepping into the room with the easy grace she'd noticed the night he'd rescued her.

She hadn't known him then.

He'd simply been a man who'd said he was there to help.

Now, he was a man who'd saved her life, who'd believed the truth about Ruby's death, who'd devoted himself to proving that Ruby had been murdered and to finding the person who'd killed her.

And her heart soared when she saw him—every single time—lifting toward him the same way a flower lifted toward the sun. She could feel it happening, and she was helpless to stop it.

She didn't even think she wanted to.

"How are you holding up?" he asked, dropping down beside her.

"Great. But that's easy to do since all I'm doing is waiting."

"Sometimes waiting is the hardest part," he said.

"Have you heard from Adam?"

"He and Bo will be here in five minutes. Depending on what Bo says, we may send two people with him to locate your car. Three will stay here with you."

"Are you going to be one of the three?" she asked, and she wasn't embarrassed by the neediness in her voice, by the way she longed to know he would be around if trouble *did* come.

"Do you want me to be?"

"Yes." She said it simply, because it was simple.

He asked. She told the truth.

No hedging. No pretending. No hoping that what she said wouldn't be used to manipulate and use her.

"I was hoping you'd say that," he responded, sliding his arm around her waist and pulling her into his side. Being there felt warm and comfortable and right, and she rested her head against his shoulder, feeling firm muscle and soft cotton against her cheek.

"Do you think Ian is going to show?" she asked.

"I think someone will. There's no way this is just Bo trying to protect his family. He could have asked for protection for them at any time, and we'd have given it. And he could have easily brought Adam to your car without coming here."

"So he's still working with The Organization?"

"Or they're using something to manipulate him. Like his family. Radley was right when he said that would be Bo's vulnerability. He might be the kind of guy I prefer to avoid, but he does seem to care about his wife and his kids."

"How old are his children?"

"His son is fourteen, and his daughter is seventeen."

"So prime age for human trafficking? The Organization probably would have noticed that."

"I hadn't thought about it that way, but you're right. His kids would be easy to sell on the black market." He stood, pulling her up with him. "I need to call Sheriff Johnson."

"Do you think Bo's kids have been kidnapped?"

"I don't know, but I'm going to ask the sheriff to look around the shipping crates. He's had officers do triweekly patrols of the area, but I don't know when they've been out last. If The Organization were going to try to hide a couple of kids, that seems like as good a place as any."

"I hope they're in Portland with Bo's in-laws. If they're not, I hope the sheriff finds them quickly. I was terrified when I was in that crate. I hate to imagine two young kids being there."

"Or all the kids that came before them?" he asked, and she thought about the kids who'd been reported missing by business owners in Newcastle. She thought of how alone they must have felt and how scared. She knew how it felt to be tied up in the dark, knowing that no one would be looking for her. She knew the feeling of desperation and terror.

"Do you think they'll be recovered?" she asked.

"I hope that we'll find information on the medical clinic's computers that will give us an idea of where they were shipped. I'm assuming a crime syndicate the size of The Organization must keep records of their successes and their failures. If we don't find any, our only hope is that someone in The Organization will talk. Maybe give us an idea of where to start looking. One way or another, we're not going to give up on finding them and bringing them home." He glanced at this watch and frowned. "I need to get back downstairs. Stay here, okay?"

"I planned on it," she assured him.

"No matter what, okay? Because things could get crazy, and I don't want you to get caught in the cross fire of a gun battle."

"Do you think it's going to come to that?"

"I think I don't want to take any chances with your life. Promise me you'll stay in here unless one of us comes to get you?"

She could have refused. She could think of a dozen scenarios where she might feel it necessary to escape on her own. But she was looking in his face and into his eyes. She could see his concern, and she couldn't deny him what he'd asked.

"I promise," she said, and he smiled, leaning down to kiss her gently. Sweetly. A million promises in that one light and beautiful touch.

And then he was walking away, closing the door, closing her back in with her fear and her thoughts.

She sat down. On the floor in the middle of the room.

Waiting.

Only this time she prayed. For Bo and his family. For the teenagers who had been kidnapped and sold. For the Special Crimes Unit.

For Sam.

Because he mattered, and because she cared, and because when this was over, she really did want to see where the future would bring them.

Downstairs, a door opened and closed.

Voices drifted into the silence.

Muted, but audible. Quiet and indistinct.

Bo must have arrived.

She could hear chairs scraping on the kitchen floor, smell fresh coffee rising through the vents.

She wanted to go downstairs and hear the conversation, find out for herself what Bo had to say. But she'd made her promise, and she wasn't going to break it. Ten minutes passed, then twenty, and the door opened and closed again.

For a few minutes afterward, she could hear faint voices. She imagined Sam, Wren and Radley standing in the kitchen, discussing the case. They'd given up the comfort of their homes and the presence of their families to be in Newcastle, and she knew they were as anxious for this to be over as she was. Had their meeting with Bo gone well? Were they happy with the information they'd received from him?

Minutes ticked by and the house grew quiet, silence settling like a thick and comfortable blanket. No chaos. No danger. No bullets whizzing by. Just those quiet voices slowly fading, the world fading with them.

Her eyes drifted closed, and she opened them again, certain this wasn't the end of it, that the night wouldn't end in quiet voices and gentle sleep.

Ten minutes. Twenty. Thirty.

She stared at the clock until her body grew heavy and her mind was numb, and then she grabbed a blanket and pillow from the bed, lay on the floor and stared at it more.

Because she didn't believe the peace any more than she should have believed Jarrod's lies.

This time, though, time passed, the silence

continued and she slowly relaxed, drifting away on disjointed thoughts and velvety darkness and the soft, sweet sound of peace.

Sam expected trouble the same way he expected the sun to rise and the tide to flow. It was coming, but he didn't have a chart to look at to figure out the time or a handy website that could help him calculate it.

He had gut instinct, and it was saying soon.

He paced from the kitchen into the living room and back, his gun holstered but available, his nerves alive with adrenaline. It had been nearly two hours since Bo's visit, and there'd been no call from Adam or Wren, no indication that Bo had been telling the truth when he'd said he would lead them to Ella's vehicle.

Sam was certain he knew where the vehicle was.

Bo'd offered a convincing story, explaining in detail the way he'd hot-wired the old station wagon. His description had been thorough, and Sam had been nearly convinced that he'd done the job. When he'd pulled a laptop from a duffel he'd been carrying, any doubt had disappeared.

It was a beat-up and well-loved machine, a few flower decals stuck haphazardly to the exterior. Bo had found it in a box in the back seat of the station wagon, and he'd removed it before he'd abandoned the car.

When he'd been asked why, he'd had no explanation, except that he hadn't wanted Ian to have it. It had seemed too personal of an item to be lost to him or The Organization.

Sam hadn't believed that story, and he hadn't been convinced that Bo was going to lead Adam and Wren to the vehicle. He'd been too vague about the location, describing trees and barns and an abandoned house that could have been in any town in the country.

Wren hadn't believed him, either. Sam was sure of that. She'd gone along with the charade anyway, because they wanted Bo to tip his hat and show his hand.

The sooner the better.

Sam hadn't been lying when he'd told Ella that waiting was sometimes the most difficult thing to do. He liked it about as much as he liked cabbage and kale: not at all.

"You can stop pacing anytime you want," Honor muttered, her head bent over the laptop, her shoulders taut. He'd been working with her for a couple of years, and he'd never known her to be tense or anxious. She seemed to face every job with a mixture of confidence and enthusiasm.

Right now, she seemed worried, a frown line

marring her smooth brow, dark circles beneath her eyes.

"Sorry." He dropped into a seat across the table from her, watching as she typed something, waited, typed again.

"You can stop staring anytime you want," she muttered without looking up from her work. This was definitely not Honor-like. She didn't gripe, didn't snap and didn't expect people to do things her way. She certainly had never expected anyone in the unit to make her job easier or to accommodate her idiosyncrasies. He'd seen her work her computer magic in the middle of a boardroom teeming with loud people. No way was his staring impacting her ability to work.

"What's wrong?" he asked, and she sighed, rubbing the back of her neck and pushing away from the table.

"They cleaned it. The files are gone. Or, at least, on the surface they seem to be. They're still there. It's just going to take me a lot longer to access them."

"We have time."

"We do, but what about the next kid that The Organization plans to kidnap? Does she or he?"

"You can't protect the next victim by accessing those computer files sooner. You know that, right?"

"Of course I do, but I have a superhero complex, Sam. I think I can save everyone. If I work hard enough and try hard enough and put enough into it. Haven't I mentioned that yet?" He thought she was only partially kidding, and he watched as she walked to the carafe and poured more coffee into her nearly empty cup.

"Want some sugar with that?"

"No. I'm taking this hit for straight caffeine. Not for flavor." She took a sip and shuddered. "About as nasty as I thought."

"Sugar is a good energy boost," he reminded her, and she shrugged, dropping back into her seat and staring at the screen again.

"At least I know one thing for sure," she commented.

"What's that?"

"Bo's story isn't completely on the up-and-up. If he moved the car, found the laptop and took it with him, he also had to be the one to clean this. I don't think he has the knowledge for that. Even if he does, why do it?"

"Unless there was something on it that would incriminate him, he wouldn't have had a reason."

"That's my point. What could possibly be on Ruby's computer that would incriminate him?"

"Information about his money laundering?"

"We already know about that."

"A list of the kidnapping victims? Maybe he's more involved than he wants us to think. Or, maybe, the computer was wiped clean by someone else in The Organization." That seemed the most likely explanation.

"Right. That's what I'm thinking." She typed again, her fingers flying rapidly over the keys. She looked exhausted, her skin pale.

"You look tired, Honor," he said, hoping to get a reaction from her. Maybe a comment about how that was just what every woman wanted to hear.

Instead, she shrugged.

"It's been a long week, and I'm starting to feel tired."

"Starting? You've been burning the candle at both ends since we arrived in town. Teaching classes and trying to access files from the clinic's database."

"That's not hard work. Not like what you and the rest of the team are doing."

"Why do you say that?"

She stopped typing and met his eyes, and for a moment, he saw something he'd never seen before—doubt, vulnerability, fear.

"Because it's true," she finally responded. "Physically, this type of work is as about as draining as sitting on a lawn chair at the pool."

"It's mentally exhausting, though," he reminded her, and she shrugged again.

"What is this conversation about, Sam?"

"I'm worried about you."

"Don't be. I can take care of myself."

"You'll take care of yourself better after a good night's sleep."

"Maybe, but I'm not going to get one until I figure this…" Her voice trailed off, her eyes focused on the screen. "Uh-oh."

"What?"

"See this?" She tapped the screen, pointing to a long strand of numbers and symbols.

"Yes."

"It looks like a tracking code of some sort. Someone from a remote location could use it to get the coordinates of the device and find it if it went missing. It's not organic to the machine. As in—it's not built into the system. I found it mixed in with some other files that were pretty well hidden." She turned off the computer, frowning as she eyed the black screen.

"What other files?"

"One is a list of names, birth dates and dates missing."

"Dates missing? That's what it says?"

"Yes. I'd show you, but I don't want to turn on the machine again. Not until I figure out how to remove the tracking bug."

"It can't be used when the machine is off?"

"Probably not."

"You don't sound very confident."

"I'm not. I've never seen the code before, and I've seen a lot of code. I've created a lot of code." She smoothed her hair, took another sip of coffee. "Unfortunately, I've had the computer running for two hours. That's two hours someone could have used to figure out our location."

"We'd better get Radley," he suggested.

"Get me for what?" he said, stepping into the room.

Honor explained quickly, skirting over the technical aspects of what she'd found and getting right to the point. When she finished, Radley nodded and strode to the back door. "I'd better run an exterior patrol. I want to make sure the perimeter is clear. Once I've assessed that, we can come up with a plan for getting Ella out of here."

That was exactly what Sam had been thinking—get her out, get her to Boston, hide her away until this was over.

"Am I more useful here or following you?" Honor asked, pulling her firearm and checking the chamber. Sam could feel her tension, just like he could feel his own.

They'd known trouble could come. They just hadn't imagined that they'd be drawing it to them, sending out a beacon and a signal to guide it on its way.

"Stay here," Radley said. "I'll text if I see anything unusual."

He opened the back door and slipped outside, fading into the shadows so quickly Sam wouldn't have known he was there if he hadn't seen him go.

"How does he do that?" Honor asked, closing the door and turning the lock.

"What?"

"The disappearing thing. One minute he's there, the next he's not. I find it disconcerting."

"I find it useful. He can get into or out of almost any situation without being noticed. On nights like tonight, that's an important attribute," he responded, crossing the room and checking the window above the sink. He knew there was no easy way for an intruder to get in, but he needed to be sure that every access point was secure. Just the way Ella had earlier.

Ella...

Yeah. He couldn't stop thinking about her, about the way her eyes had widened when he'd appeared in the kitchen, the quick flash of surprise followed by a warm sweep of pleasure.

Because she was there, and he was, and there was nothing nicer than being in a room with her.

Those were dangerous thoughts, and he'd acknowledged that days ago. He'd also acknowledged that a little danger in his life wasn't always a bad thing.

If it affected his judgment, though, if it kept him from doing his job, it would be a problem.

He wasn't going to let that happen.

He walked into the living room, moving across the oversize space, his heart thrumming with adrenaline. He'd trained for this kind of thing. He knew how to face danger and how to neutralize it. He knew as much as he needed to stay alive and to protect the people around him.

Knowing how to be what Ella needed, that was going to be more difficult. But he'd like to try. The way he saw things, God had put them in each other's lives at just the time when they each needed it most. He wanted to explore what that might mean for now and for the future. Later, though. When they didn't have danger breathing down their necks and an organization of thugs hunting them down.

His cell phone buzzed, and he pulled it out, glancing at the number. It was Radley—his text flashing across the screen.

Found a vehicle parked on the road half a mile away. License plate matches the partial the sheriff got off the car that ran him off the road.

The sheriff had found a match to the partial, but the vehicle had been reported stolen months ago after it disappeared from the parking garage at the medical clinic.

No way to know who had taken it, who'd been driving it when it had run the sheriff's vehicle into the river or who'd parked it half a mile away. But Sam could make a reasonable assumption.

Ian Wade had access to the parking garage and plenty of people willing to do his dirty work. If he'd needed a backup vehicle that couldn't be traced to him, stealing one was a good way to go.

His phone buzzed again as another text came through.

Interesting stuff here. Looks like the back seat of the car is filled with suitcases.

How many? Sam typed.

Enough to go away and be gone a long time. I'd say it's getting a little hot for our guy, and he's trying to get to a cooler location.

Contact Wren. See if she can get an emergency warrant.

Will do, Radley responded.

* * *

And then the world exploded. Glass shattering. Smoke billowing up and pouring in through the broken window. Fire eating at the thick curtains and the world shaking as another explosion rocked the house.

"We need to get Ella and get out!" Honor shouted, but he was already running, racing up the stairs toward Ella's room.

THIRTEEN

She felt the first explosion.

It shook her from sleep, drove her into consciousness.

She was up on her feet, confused and disoriented when she heard the second—the sound reverberating through the room, shaking the foundation of the house.

Smoke billowed up from the room below, and she ran for the door, remembered what Sam had asked. What she had promised.

Her hand was on the doorknob, her heart thudding wildly, her brain screaming that she should forget the promise and get out. Now!

The door flew open, the knob ripped from her hand as Sam bounded into the room. He didn't speak. He didn't need to. The house was still shaking, and she wondered how long it would hold together before the damage from the explosion brought it down.

Sam grabbed her hand and pulled her out of the room.

She was surprised when he didn't race for the stairs, didn't head straight for the front door. They could have made it easily. She could see that. No flames near the stairs or the front foyer. Nothing preventing them from opening the door and running out into the darkness.

But Honor was at the other end of the hall, struggling with a window that opened out to the side yard.

"Give me a hand, Sam!" she shouted, and Sam dragged Ella toward her.

She tried to pull away, desperately yanking against his hold.

"There's a front door! That will be quicker," she nearly yelled, her fear coming out in a burst of frantic words and short breaths.

"Someone set off those explosions. Whoever it was will be watching the doors, waiting for us to exit the house," Sam replied, giving her hand a reassuring squeeze before letting it drop.

He was calm.

She was panicked.

"If we go out the front door, we're going to be moving targets for a sniper's bullet," he continued, saying it casually as if it were an everyday situation, a predictable one.

"If we jump out a window, we're going to

have broken legs and no way of escaping when this house falls down," she responded.

"We've got that covered," Honor said, opening a window seat and pulling out a rope ladder. "Easy-peasy. We'll be done in a blink of an eye."

"If the window ever opens," Ella muttered, not sure she liked the idea of climbing down a rope ladder when the guy who bombed the house was lurking outside.

She liked the idea of staying inside even less, and when Sam finally wrestled the window open, she was relieved to feel the frigid air blowing against her cheeks.

He attached the ladder to the sill and dropped it, the rope swishing as it unraveled.

"I'll go first," he said. "You're second, Ella. Then Honor."

"What if…?" *What if the house collapses before the last person descends?* The question almost tripped off her tongue. She held it back, because the more time Sam wasted explaining things, the less likely they'd all make it out alive.

The house shook again—a quick quiver that made her heart jump and her mind go numb.

"Let's go!" Sam shouted, climbing out and scrambling down. Moving so quickly she barely saw him go. At the top and then at the bottom, and it was suddenly her turn.

"You can do this, Ella," Honor said, as if Ella

being afraid was her greatest concern, as if she wasn't calculating the time it would take for a terrified person to make it to the ground. As if she wasn't wondering if there'd be enough time to do the same.

And maybe she wasn't, because she leaned out the window, looked down. "It's not that far. Just take your time and take it one step after another. You'll be down before you know it."

"I'll be quick," Ella promised, climbing over the window ledge, her heart thumping wildly.

She didn't look down.

She didn't dare.

She was afraid if she did, she'd freeze, stuck at the top and blocking Honor's escape.

Her legs shook, but she managed to find the first rung and the second. Feet first. Then hands. Easy. But not as quick as she wanted to be. She knew Sam was at the bottom, that he was waiting for her to clamber down and that if she fell, he'd try to catch her.

Try, because the house had a raised foundation and a walkout basement. They were on the second floor, but they were three-stories high. If she fell from that height, the likelihood that he'd be able to stop her momentum and keep her from being injured was slim to none. That wasn't fun or cool. Neither was Ella taking her time and letting Honor's life hang in the balance.

She'd felt the foundation shake.

She knew it had been damaged.

Every second she wasted was a second closer to the structure caving in.

Another explosion rocked the house, and she screamed, losing her grip as a piece of gutter crashed by a few inches away. She tried to grab on to the rope again, but she was already falling, flailing, searching for a way to stop herself.

Sam caught Ella easily, setting her down and turning his attention to the window again. Honor was already out, moving quickly, climbing down like she'd spent her life doing it.

When her feet hit the ground, they were off, racing toward the tree line, as a fourth explosion rocked the ground.

Not big explosions.

These were the kind created by amateurs. Usually kids who thought it would be funny to make a bomb based off internet instructions. More bark than bite, the bombs could damage structures and kill people, but usually ended up blowing a trash can or Dumpster to smithereens, instead.

Of course, this wasn't a kid playing a game. This was an adult with deadly intent. Ian wasn't playing around, and he wasn't taking chances.

He wanted to take them out, and he was using whatever he thought necessary to do it.

How many bombs would he set off?

And was he alone?

That was the more important question.

The spacing of the bombs made Sam think he was. Otherwise, he'd have been able to set them off simultaneously. Front, back, sides. Hoping that the house would collapse. Knowing that if it didn't, his prey would race outside to escape the smoke and the possibility of the structure caving in.

Just like they had.

He'd expected them to exit through the front door.

He'd left that route open.

It wouldn't take him long to figure out they'd found a different way.

Sam had his hand around Ella's wrist, and he was running at full speed. She somehow managed to keep up, taking two or three steps for every one of his. She couldn't keep that pace forever, but she seemed determined to try.

Or, maybe, she was just determined not to slow them down.

He'd been surprised at how quickly she'd climbed out the window. She was afraid of heights. She'd admitted that, and the window of the log cabin had been higher than the apartment balcony.

She'd managed, though, and she'd have made it down quickly, even if she hadn't fallen. The fact that she had had shaved six years off Sam's life. He'd been certain he'd felt gray hair sprouting as he'd somehow managed to break her fall.

They made it to the trees, and he slowed, listening to the sudden silence. No forest creatures roaming around. No crickets chirping. Nothing but a thick quiet filled with expectation.

"We should head to the road," Honor whispered. "Wren and Adam can pick us up there."

"You contacted them?" he responded, glancing over his shoulder, his attention on the house and the small flames that were bright against the foundation.

The fire would be out before fire crews arrived. Whether or not the foundation was damaged enough for the house to be condemned was something structural engineers and the fire marshal would have to decide.

"Of course," Honor said, moving to the left and toward the only access road to the property. "I called while I was trying to open the window. Wren said they were already on the way back. Bo took them on a nice merry little drive, and she got tired of it. She told him she'd had enough, and they were done."

"I'm not sure the road is the place to be," he said, the hair on his arms suddenly standing up.

He stopped, pulling Ella with him, listening again.

A twig snapped, the sound reverberating through the forest, and Honor froze, suddenly understanding what Sam already did—they weren't alone.

"Radley?" she mouthed through the darkness, her face a pale oval.

He shook his head.

Radley moved silently.

If he were there, he wouldn't be heard. Not until he wanted to be.

Another branch snapped, this one closer, and he started moving again. Quietly. Quickly. Ella right beside him, hand in his. Honor just a few steps ahead, leading them deeper into the trees instead of toward the road.

She understood now…just how close they all were to dying. One misstep, one loud noise, and gunfire would erupt. Whether or not Wade could see his target wouldn't matter. He'd failed at his plan to flush them out and into the line of fire. Now, he'd do whatever he could to make certain he succeeded in his goal. Revenge, retaliation, retribution. Whatever word was put to it, it meant the same—murder.

Wade had his car packed, and he was ready

to start a new life, but first he wanted to end the old one by killing the people who had cost him everything.

The distant sound of sirens drifted through the forest, and Sam knew Wade heard it, that he was probably getting desperate to finish what he'd started. He was an arrogant man, one who'd gotten away with his crimes for years. He wasn't expecting to be caught, but he wouldn't stay around waiting for it to happen.

He'd act, and then he'd run.

Sam frowned, the early-warning system he'd acquired from years of working as a law enforcement officer going off, yelling for his attention. Demanding it.

Telling him he wasn't safe.

They weren't safe.

Telling him to get down, take cover, wait.

Honor was just ahead, moving through a towering pine forest, moonlight providing just enough light to make her an easy target.

Behind him, another branch snapped, and he could feel the eyes of the hunter. Feel them like he felt the cold on his skin. A safety cocked, the sound as unmistakable as a lush flower in the desert.

"Get down!" he shouted, and he saw Honor duck as he tackled Ella to the ground, gunfire exploding through the darkness.

FOURTEEN

She wasn't dead, but she would be if Sam didn't move.

He was a heavy weight, driving her face into the loamy earth and forcing the air from her lungs.

"Sam?" she gasped, and when he didn't respond, she knew.

That he was hurt.

Shot.

Needed help.

She managed to squeeze out from beneath him, wiggling into thick brambles, the sound of someone screaming discordant background noise to her frantically pounding heart.

"Sam?" she said again, feeling for his pulse and finding it. Steady and slow. Just like it should be.

But he still wasn't moving, and she was terrified.

"Everyone okay?" Radley called, moving

through the woods loudly for a change, his footsteps matched by the frantic panicked cries of the man he was escorting. Ian Wade didn't look nearly as arrogant and perfect as the day she'd met him. He didn't look like the sorrowful boyfriend or the busy doctor. He looked like a criminal, his wrists in cuffs, blood dripping from a wound in his upper arm.

"*I'm* not okay, you idiot!" he howled. "I'm bleeding, and if you don't stop and render aid, I'm going to sue you and everyone you work with."

"That would be a lot of people, Doctor," Radley said, stretching out the last word as if he wanted to remind Ian of just how far he'd fallen.

"I don't care how many people it is, it's happening. You have no right to treat me like this."

"Like what?" Honor asked, popping up from behind a clump of shoulder-high bushes. "A criminal?"

"Sam is injured," Ella broke in, her voice trembling with fear, her hands shaking as she tried to find the wound.

She ran her hands up his arms, slid them along the column of his neck, felt warm blood oozing from somewhere.

His head?

No, please, Lord. Don't let it be that, she prayed silently, urgently. Because she couldn't imagine anyone surviving a bullet to the head. She couldn't imagine him opening his eyes and telling her that everything was going to be okay.

She couldn't imagine life without him, either.

She couldn't imagine going back to her house and picking up where she'd left off—writing her articles, sticking close to home, doing safe and easy things because they didn't make her afraid.

"Please don't die," she whispered in his ear.

A light flashed on, and the forest was illuminated. Green pine needles, golden leaves and Sam lying motionless and silent, blood seeping from his temple and dripping onto the ground.

Her heart dropped, her throat tightened and tears she'd been holding back for days slid down her cheeks. She didn't try to stop them. She didn't care who saw. Out of the billions of people on earth, she'd found the one who could have mattered.

Who *did* matter.

For always.

And he was lying on the ground bleeding, because he'd been willing to give everything to protect her.

"Sam!" Honor yelled, dropping down beside Ella, the light in her hand. "Did you check his pulse?"

"Yes. He's alive, but…" She gestured to the

blood, her words too muffled with tears to be intelligible.

"Call for an ambulance!" Honor shouted.

Ella wasn't sure who she was shouting at, but she grabbed her phone and dialed, the sound of sirens growing louder.

An operator answered on the second ring, and Ella gave the situation and location, repeating questions that she was asked so that Honor could hear.

"Is he breathing?" she asked, and Honor nodded.

"Steady pulse. Bullet wound to the right temple. We'll need a trauma team, so ask for Life-Flight to the nearest level one trauma hospital. Do we know where that is?"

"We'll need LifeFlight," she told the dispatcher. "He's been shot in the head."

She said it calmly, as if it weren't important, as if her heart weren't breaking, as if everything that had happened to Sam weren't her fault. He'd saved her life. If he'd sacrificed his own doing it, she didn't know how she could live with that. He was a one-in-a-million kind of guy. The world shouldn't lose a man like him.

She didn't want to lose him.

"Sam?" She touched his cheek, her voice breaking.

"Tell them to send the ambulance STAT!"

Honor shouted to be heard above the sirens, tugging off her jacket and pressing it against the bleeding wound. "He's alive. I'd like to keep it that way!"

"So would I," Sam said, the words sluggish but clear. "So how about you lower your voice before the sound breaks my skull?"

"Sam!" Ella shouted, so surprised, so relieved, tears pooled in her eyes. "You're okay!"

"If okay is having a sledgehammer hitting me in the head every couple of seconds, yeah. I'm fine." He finally opened his eyes, looked into her face. Smiled gently. "Don't cry, sweetheart. I'm fine."

"How is having a sledgehammer hitting you in the head fine?" she said, sniffing back tears, wiping them from her face, because he was going to be okay. She was certain of that. Just like she was certain that when this was over, and she returned home, he'd be the first person she thought of every morning and the last one she thought of every night.

"You're here. I'm here. In my opinion, life is good." He closed his eyes again, and Honor leaned over him, giving his shoulder a brisk shake.

"Hey, Romeo, don't fall sleep and leave your ladylove to worry."

He opened his eyes again. "Did I mention I've got a headache?"

"Yes. Stay awake anyway. If you die, I'll have to take up your slack on the team. That won't be cool." Her voice was shaking, and she looked as relieved as Ella felt, her face drained of color, her eyes bright. She tore strips of fabric from her jacket and used them to bind Sam's wound.

"There. At least you won't bleed to death. I'm going to find the ambulance. With the amount of sirens I'm hearing, I figure there must be one around."

"How about Wade?" Sam asked, his focus on Ella, his gaze unwavering.

"Sam, you were just shot in the head, I don't think you should worry about anything but staying conscious."

"I wasn't shot in the head. The bullet grazed my temple." He touched the spot and grimaced, then levered up so he was sitting. "I'm probably going to need some stitches, but I've had worse."

"Good thing you have such a hard head. Otherwise, you'd probably need a lot more than that," Radley commented, moving closer, Ian still mumbling and complaining beside him.

"I appreciate your overwhelming sympathy. I'll make sure to remember it the next time you're injured," Sam said, and Radley grinned.

"You're obviously going to be just fine. Wren

texted me and told me to bring our perp to the road. The sheriff is waiting to take him into custody. Since you're planning to live, I'll go ahead and do that."

"Custody? For what?" Ian shouted, and Sam winced.

"You might want to take him now," he suggested.

"I didn't do anything! I was just walking through the woods, minding my own business, and the next thing I knew, you shot me!" Ian continued, as if Sam hadn't spoken.

"You know, Doc," Radley said, "that's a really good story. Keep telling it while we walk, because you *are* going to be arrested, and you *are* going to be booked and you're going to jail for a very long time. There's not a whole lot you can say to stop it, but if you'd like to give us some information about the way you and your friends operate, hand over information about what you did with the teens who've gone missing, then maybe we'll have room to discuss the terms of your prison stay."

"I have a lawyer. I demand an opportunity to speak with him."

"As soon as we can locate him, we'll hook you up." Radley led Ian away, and the sirens shut off. The world suddenly quiet again.

And it was just Ella and Sam, sitting in the darkness, looking into each other's eyes.

"I'm so glad you're okay," she whispered, wrapping her arms around him. Gently, because he'd been injured, and she didn't want to hurt him more.

"Me, too," he murmured, his lips brushing her hair, then her cheek, then her lips. Softly. Tenderly. Just like before, and she could have cried with the beauty of it.

She broke away, breathless and touched and so very glad to be in this place with this man. "You should lie down until the ambulance crew arrives," she suggested, and he smiled the way he always did. Open and honest and real.

"I have a better idea," he responded, getting to his feet, steadier than she'd expected. Stronger than she'd thought he could be after losing so much blood.

"Sam, really, this isn't a good idea." She grabbed his hand, trying to stop him.

"I think it's a great idea. We'll go find the ambulance. I'll get a few stitches and a few days of leave from Wren because of it." He squeezed her hand and started walking, heading toward the lights that flashed through the trees.

"Medical leave is probably well deserved considering the fact that you were shot."

"Grazed," he corrected. "And usually I'd hate

taking forced leave. I'm not so keen on sitting around my house waiting to get cleared to go back to work. This time, though, I can think of ways to pass the time."

"Like?"

"Visiting you in Charlotte, seeing your house and your writing and you…enjoying the place that makes you most happy."

"That would be wonderful, but there's something you need to know, Sam."

He stopped then, turning so they were face-to-face.

"If you're afraid, I understand. If you want me to stay away for a while, I can do that," he said, his tone as gentle as a butterfly's kiss. "Whatever you want, I'll give it to you, El. You're everything I didn't know I was looking for, and I'm so thankful God brought you into my life."

"What I want," she murmured, stepping close, laying her hand against his jaw. He was a head taller, and she levered up on her tiptoes, looking straight into his eyes, wanting him to see everything she felt, everything she meant. All the truth of her words. "Is to tell you that you are the place where I'm most happy. When I'm with you, I'm home."

For a moment, he didn't speak, didn't move. Just stood looking into her eyes, searching her face.

Studying it the way she thought an artist would study his subject—as if every detail mattered.

Then he leaned down to kiss her again. With passion, promise and joy.

When he finally broke away, he brushed moisture from her cheeks, his palms calloused, warm and as familiar as sunrise.

"I hope those are happy tears," he said quietly.

"The happiest," she admitted.

"Then let's go find that ambulance crew. I don't know how you feel, but I'm ready to get out of here and get on with life. Wherever that leads us."

She smiled at that and at him, taking his hand, kissing his knuckles.

"Us? I like the sound of that," she responded.

He slid his arm around her waist, his fingers splayed against her side.

And they walked through pine needles and moonlight, heading for the emergency lights and emergency crews and whatever future God planned for them. Together.

EPILOGUE

Winter in Boston was everything Ella had expected: snow and cold, ice and wind. She saw and felt all those things as she stepped outside, walking into the hustle and bustle of the busy airport sidewalk.

Sounds and activity and people.

So much of everything.

She could have cowered away, scurrying to some quiet corner to wait for her ride.

She stood in the middle of it instead, people moving around her, suitcases thumping on the ground.

And she was okay.

Not afraid like she would have been months ago.

Not nervous or worried or anxious.

If Ruby was here, she'd be proud of the progress Ella had made, and of the adventure she was on. A weeklong stay in a bed-and-breakfast in Peabody to celebrate testifying at Ian

Wade's trial. He'd been convicted and sentenced to twenty years in prison. Turns out, Ruby had been onto Ian, and the dates on her computer aligned with when the teenagers went missing. That evidence alone would have been enough to implicate Ian, which is why he murdered her. Several high-level members of The Organization had also been arrested and, in exchange for plea deals and lesser sentences, had offered files and information that, along with Ruby's notes, had led to the recovery of ten of the missing teenagers. Sam had said the FBI was hopeful the rest would eventually be located and freed.

Sam.

He'd been a bright spot in a very dark time.

He'd sat beside her while she'd waited to testify. He'd told her over and over again that things would be okay.

And he'd been right.

Things were okay.

The Organization's Newcastle cell had dismantled. Bo had been offered immunity for his testimony, and he and his family had entered witness protection. The medical clinic was under new management, and the small town was back to being the serene and peaceful place it had been before The Organization arrived.

And Ella…

She still missed Ruby. Every day, but she saw

the bigger part of God's plan. The way that He had used the tragedy of Ruby's death to bring about the destruction of a crime syndicate that would have killed many more people.

It still hurt, but Ella imagined that Ruby would have been happy with the outcome.

She sighed, rolling her luggage closer to the curb and eyeing the drivers waiting near their vehicles. She had several hours to kill before she had to get ready for dinner with Sam, but she was still anxious to get to the bed-and-breakfast. Sam had to work late, but had promised to send a car to pick her up. She didn't see a driver holding a sign with her name, but she knew Sam hadn't forgotten. He never forgot his promises.

He'd visited her in North Carolina half a dozen times, coming for long weekends and staying in hotels nearby. And they'd done all the things he'd said they would the night he'd been shot, visiting her favorite places, spending long evenings at her house. She'd even shared her current writing projects with him, allowing him to read over her shoulder while she worked.

After the trial, she'd told him it was her turn to make the trip. He'd seemed surprised and touched. She supposed that was because he knew just how hard adventures still were for her.

"But you'd want this for me, Ruby. Wouldn't

you?" she whispered, imagining the words carrying up to Heaven and reaching her cousin's ears.

"She would," Sam responded, and she whirled around.

"Sam!" she cried, throwing herself into his arms. "I thought you couldn't make it."

"There was a meeting. A long boring one. When Wren found out you and I had a dinner date, she said I could skip it. So I'm here."

"And I look like I just spent a few hours traveling," she responded, running her hand over her hair. "If I'd known you were going to meet me here, I'd have freshened up before the plane landed."

"You look beautiful. Like always," he responded, kissing her, and then grabbing the handle of her suitcase. "I parked in the garage. I was hoping I'd make it in time to surprise you in the airport, but traffic was a bear."

"Surprising me here is just as good. Actually, you surprising me anywhere is good."

He grinned. "I'm glad you think so. I had an idea."

"What kind of idea?" she asked as she followed him across a busy street and into a quieter parking garage.

"One that includes dinner and firelight and a

horse-drawn carriage. It's going to require another hour of travel, though."

"An hour of travel with you?"

"Of course. I'm not going to send you off by yourself when you just arrived." He smiled, and her heart responded—filling up with love for him. "There's a farm outside Boston," he continued. "This time of year, there are Christmas lights and bonfires. They serve dinner in a 19th-century barn that's been converted to a small restaurant."

"That sounds wonderful," she responded. "This is wonderful. Being with you here. In the place you live and work. It makes me happy. Dinner at a beautiful farm will be an unexpected bonus to an already fantastic evening."

"I'm glad you feel that way, Ella," he said, stopping beside a dark sedan and popping the trunk.

"What way?"

"Happy to be here with me." He put her suitcase in the trunk, then turned to face her again. "Because I've been thinking about our situation."

"I didn't realize we had a situation," she said, looking into his beautiful, familiar eyes. Life with him was so much fuller and brighter and more wonderful than she'd ever imagine it could be.

"What did you think we had?"

"A relationship?"

"We do, and it's a great one, but this long-distance thing. It's not working for me."

"I didn't know it was upsetting you so much," she said, her heart sinking.

"It isn't upsetting me. I just want more, Ella. I want to see you every day. Not every few weeks. I want to kiss you goodbye before I leave for work, and I want to kiss you hello when I return."

"Sam—"

"I know this isn't romantic. I'm not that kind of guy. It's not flowers and candlelight and crowds of people looking on. It's just me and you standing in a public place, and me not being able to wait for the horse-drawn carriage ride like Wren suggested." He pulled a small box from his pocket and opened it, revealing a beautiful sapphire-and-diamond ring. "I love you, Ella. I want to spend my life with you. Will you marry me?"

"You're wrong," she responded, her voice tight with tears of joy that filled her eyes and slipped down her cheeks. "This is romantic, and you are that kind of guy. My kind of guy. I love you, too. Of course I'll marry you."

He smiled, slipping the ring on her finger and wiping the tears from her cheeks.

"You are the most amazing person I have ever met, Ella," he whispered against her lips. "I can't wait to call you my wife."

And then he kissed her, sealing their love and their future together. A brand-new adventure, and Ella could almost hear Ruby's joyful laughter.

* * * * *

Dear Reader,

I hope you're enjoying the *FBI: Special Crimes Unit* series as much as I am! Writing these stories has given me an opportunity to explore some of the darker aspects of life. It has also given me an opportunity to explore the most beautiful. Every day, I read news reports about the terrible things that go on in the world. These things challenge me to be kinder, to worker harder and to extend more grace. The world needs more of what God has offered—peace and restoration. Through His abundant grace and mercy, we learn to offer the same to those around us. In *Gone*, Ella and Sam have both been through challenges in life. Their faith is what pulls them through, guiding them to have hearts of forgiveness and love. I hope and pray the same for you, my friends. May the journey you're on always lead you to peace, forgiveness and grace.

I love hearing from readers. You can reach me at shirlee@shirleemccoy.com or visit me on Facebook or Instagram.

Blessings on your journey,
Shirlee McCoy

Get 4 FREE REWARDS!

We'll send you 2 FREE Books plus 2 FREE Mystery Gifts.

Love Inspired® books feature contemporary inspirational romances with Christian characters facing the challenges of life and love.

FREE Value Over $20

YES! Please send me 2 FREE Love Inspired® Romance novels and my 2 FREE mystery gifts (gifts are worth about $10 retail). After receiving them, if I don't wish to receive any more books, I can return the shipping statement marked "cancel." If I don't cancel, I will receive 6 brand-new novels every month and be billed just $5.24 for the regular-print edition or $5.74 each for the larger-print edition in the U.S., or $5.74 each for the regular-print edition or $6.24 each for the larger-print edition in Canada. That's a savings of at least 13% off the cover price. It's quite a bargain! Shipping and handling is just 50¢ per book in the U.S. and 75¢ per book in Canada*. I understand that accepting the 2 free books and gifts places me under no obligation to buy anything. I can always return a shipment and cancel at any time. The free books and gifts are mine to keep no matter what I decide.

Choose one: ☐ **Love Inspired® Romance Regular-Print** (105/305 IDN GMY4) ☐ **Love Inspired® Romance Larger-Print** (122/322 IDN GMY4)

Name (please print)

Address   Apt. #

City   State/Province   Zip/Postal Code

Mail to the **Reader Service:**
IN U.S.A.: P.O. Box 1341, Buffalo, NY 14240-8531
IN CANADA: P.O. Box 603, Fort Erie, Ontario L2A 5X3

Want to try two free books from another series? Call 1-800-873-8635 or visit www.ReaderService.com.

LI18

Get 4 FREE REWARDS!

We'll send you 2 FREE Books plus 2 FREE Mystery Gifts.

Harlequin® Heartwarming™ Larger-Print books feature traditional values of home, family, community and most of all—love.

FREE
Value Over
$20